DISHONOUR AND OBEY

Master Mercurius Mysteries
Book Three

Graham Brack

SAPERE
BOOKS

DISHONOUR AND OBEY

Published by Sapere Books.

20 Windermere Drive, Leeds, England, LS17 7UZ,
United Kingdom

saperebooks.com

ISBN: 978-1-80055-111-4

PROLOGUE

I am in my twilight years. There is no point in denying it; the evidence is there every time I try to climb a flight of stairs without something to lean on. No matter; I have arranged my life so that I can potter around my study, my bedroom and the university refectory without too much exertion; and, because my eyes are not as sharp as once they were, I leave most of the writing to my clerk, Jan van der Meer, whom I have had charity enough to retain for the better part of thirty years despite his imperfections. [Marginal note: his *many* imperfections.]

Without seeking public notice, I have kept company with many of the great men of this and other lands. I would have preferred to have been a simple professor, studying and writing here in Leiden, without the distractions of public service. In case my previous memoirs have not come to the reader's notice, permit me to explain that it all began when three young girls were abducted in Delft and the mayor sent to the University of Leiden asking for the cleverest man available to help the city fathers solve the problem, so — of course — I was sent.

Word of this must have reached the Stadhouder, William of Orange, who requested my help in the small matter of a treasonous plot against him. It was an unpleasant business made only marginally more palatable by a very substantial fee. I would not have it thought that I am avaricious, but already having money means you don't need to earn it, which would enable me to devote more time to my studies. There was never any danger that the University would pay me enough to arrive at this happy result.

I had hoped that I was quit of the Stadhouder's service after this. I was wrong.

Occasionally nitpickers and other blackguards delight in finding fault with my accounts, pointing to alleged inaccuracies and my great age as evidence that my tales are not to be relied upon. I beg to differ. I was there, and they were not. I have copious notes — somewhere — and an excellent memory for distant events. Things like the location of my slippers may be a different matter.

CHAPTER ONE

Beloved in the Lord, we are assembled here in the presence of God for the purpose of joining in marriage (name) and (name). Since we have received no lawful objections to their proposed union, let us reverently call to mind the institution, purpose, and obligations of the marriage state.

The holy bond of marriage was instituted by God himself at the very dawn of history. Making a man in his own likeness, he endowed him with many blessings and gave him dominion over all things. Moreover, God said, "It is not good for the man to be alone. I will make a helper suitable for him" (Genesis 2:18). So God created woman of man's own substance and brought her to the man. "For this reason a man will leave his father and mother and be united to his wife, and they will become one flesh" (Genesis 2:24).

Despite being an ordained minister, I have never had to say those words, because I don't have a parish. As a lecturer at the University of Leiden I have to preach occasionally, but since all our students are male the chances that two will want to marry each other are very slight. After all, if they expressed an interest in so doing they would immediately be burned at the stake as sodomites.

Neither has anyone said the words to me. I have not married. There are two reasons for this. First, I haven't had time. The life of an academic is very busy. Second, I am an ordained Catholic priest.

Yes, I know that seems a trifle odd, but I was first ordained as a minister in the Reformed Church; then, as a result of further study, the Bishop of Namur ordained me a priest, but in view of the persecutions then being visited on Catholics he instructed me to keep my ordination secret. He wanted a group of priests to call upon to form a new church if the old one were destroyed. This suited me because I am not enamoured of physical pain, and it seemed to me that the best way to avoid torture and imprisonment was not to let anyone know that I was a Catholic. There is also the little problem of losing my job if I were known to be Catholic; and I haven't actually left the Reformed Church, just joined another one.

I am bound to remark that matters have never come to that in my own country. The Dutch genius for compromise came into play, so at intervals anti-Catholic measures would be introduced but nobody would do much to enforce them. We all knew the rules. Catholic churches had to be discreet, hidden in side streets, and we must not meet outside the hours of the Divine Services.

In some cities, such as Utrecht, there was even more toleration most of the time, but at the cost of one's loyalty to the state being under question. And since it was the state that could hang you up by your thumbs in a dungeon and leave you there till you rotted, I chose not to upset it. Believe me, I've seen what the state is prepared to do to people who cross it, and while it was uncomfortable to watch I suspect it was a lot more uncomfortable for the poor wretches who were on the receiving end. There are some difficult pastoral issues that a man of the cloth must consider when a man begs you to show God's mercy and cut his throat.

In the autumn of 1674, I bade farewell to the Stadhouder and his court and returned to my chamber in Leiden, firmly resolved not to get embroiled in anything of the kind again. That Stadhouder, William III, was a nice man, pious and honest, but he seemed to regard a man's life as completely expendable when it came to defending his interests. I view things differently, especially where my own existence is concerned. I have no doubt that Heaven may be wonderful, but I am in no hurry to get there, and being cornered in dark alleys by knife-wielding fanatics is not something I want to experience too often.

Thus, for nearly two years I lived the peaceful life of a university lecturer with all that it entails. I taught, I marked, I examined, I wrote, I studied, I ate in the refectory, despite the cavalier disregard for cookery technique and elementary hygiene displayed by Albrecht the master cook, and whenever I could slip away I spent the evening in Jan Steen's inn on the Langebrug. I eat at the University for free, but it was worth a few stijvers to eat something that had not been through the burning, fiery furnace of Albrecht's oven. And Steen's beer was a cut above the average, possibly due to the unstinting quality control he practised personally every evening at some cost to his health.

One of the effects of my service to the Stadhouder was that he allowed the Rector of our University to step down, as he had been wishing to do for some time. We had not expected that he would choose to retire altogether, but he decided that he had been away from teaching for too long, so he bought a house and spent much of his time cultivating tulips. A few times a year he returned for University events or to conduct his personal study, when we would exchange some friendly words, but he seemed genuinely happy to have laid aside the burden of his office.

The new Rector was a man called Johannes Coccius, who was a philologian, but none the worse for that. He was a fair man who could always see both sides of an argument and therefore had great difficulties in deciding between them; or, indeed, in making any other decisions. The great benefit of this was that the University's governance returned to the pattern originally envisaged, namely, one in which the senior staff made their points and a collective decision was reached, with the Rector acting largely as a chairman. The concomitant problem was that these men were very reluctant to discipline their own kind, as a result of which the collective decisions were disobeyed with impunity. Thus one of my own students was expelled, reinstated, re-expelled and finally admitted to classes by the head of the school without the knowledge or agreement of the University council.

I kept myself to myself as much as I could. I was, if I remember correctly, researching a particularly interesting aspect of Aristotelian eudaimonia. One day I must finish writing it up, but the project is hampered by Van der Meer's inability to spell some of the long words that I dictate to him.

At the point that this story begins, I had just returned from a secret assignation with Albrecht's wife Mechtild. There was no vulgar purpose in this; Mechtild was robustly constructed and not comely in the conventional sense, but she had an angel's touch with pastry that delighted the soul, and for some reason she felt the need to mother me, frequently expressing concern that I might be losing weight. I was, but so was everyone who ate her husband's burnt offerings and had any sense of taste. Until I met Albrecht, I did not know that it was possible to burn soup.

So it was that from time to time Mechtild would whisper to me as she served at the refectory tables, intimating that if I came to the kitchen door at some appointed hour there might be an egg custard or cheese pie for me. It was for this reason that I ascended the stairs to my chamber with such a pie concealed in my sleeve and had just stowed it in my chest with a view to an evening treat when there was a knock at my door. When I opened it, the bedellus was standing there.

The bedellus is a species of superior janitor who carries the mace at ceremonial occasions and runs errands for the Rector. His current duty was to request my presence in the Rector's chamber at my earliest possible convenience. When I prevaricated, it was made clear that my earliest possible convenience meant at once, whatever I was doing, so I meekly followed him, mentally retracing my actions for anything dishonourable. Had someone seen me accepting the pie and informed on me? Whilst trivial in itself, it was just the sort of thing that got staff dismissed, particularly since the tribunal would all be jealous if they knew I was receiving a private supply of pastry from Mechtild; and it is in the nature of weak leaders to punish those of lower standing and leave the superiors to flaunt their lack of respect.

We walked together to the Rector's room, where the bedellus knocked and opened the door for me upon hearing the summons to enter. He stood in the doorway, making it extremely difficult to squeeze past, rather in the manner of a doorman expecting a tip, but at length I was able to gain entry and stood respectfully in front of the Rector's desk.

'Ah, Mercurius, thank you for coming so promptly.'

It seemed inappropriate to point out that his titan had required it, especially since he was still standing in the doorway. Perhaps his fat head was wedged there.

The previous Rector had been a small man, but neat and spry. This one was pasty-faced and lean. The old Rector had worn a skullcap over closely cropped grey hair; his successor had such a head of hair that opinion was divided as to whether it was a wig or not.

The Rector rummaged around his desk and produced a letter which he held with the ends of his fingers in the manner of one who has found a caterpillar in his salad. 'The Stadhouder has written to you,' he said, indicating the impression in the red wax seal in case I should suppose that he had opened it already. Coccius was a noted anti-monarchist, though quick to explain that he was unconcerned about the title that a man might have, but objected to autocracy of any kind. None of us had ever worked out where he stood on the issue of the De Witts, the brothers who had kept William of Orange from the Stadhoudership until a mob rose up and eviscerated them. The spontaneity of this action was doubtful given that everyone in The Hague knew it was planned except, apparently, their guards.

I thanked him and asked his permission to open it in his presence. This being given, I read quickly, and my heart sank. To be honest, it had started sinking when I saw the seal, because I could think of no circumstances in which the Stadhouder would write to me that did not fall under the heading of unwelcome tidings.

'The Stadhouder wishes me to attend upon him at The Hague as soon as you give me leave,' I announced. This was untrue, because the Rector's consent was not sought in the letter, but it seemed politic to suggest that it was.

Coccius rubbed his cheek. 'One must suppose that the Stadhouder would not send for you except in some great national cause, so we must not stand in your way. Please arrange for others to attend to your duties for the duration of your trip.'

I thanked him and made to leave.

'In the circumstances, I do not propose to adjust your salary.'

It had never occurred to me that he would, but why did he need to say so?

As a mark of respect, we usually left the Rector's presence backwards, bowing in the doorway and reversing out into the passageway. I had never quite mastered this action, and my rear end bore several indentations caused by the Rector's door handle. On this occasion I was spared the door handle and enjoyed the immense pleasure of hearing a sharp intake of breath from the bedellus as my rump smacked into his groin.

CHAPTER TWO

There is a barge from Leiden to The Hague, but in good weather it is as quick to walk. On the morning when I set out the weather was fine and dry, but within a couple of hours it had changed for the worse, and by the time I arrived at The Hague I was wet through.

The guards at the Binnenhof did not recognise me — there was, I suppose, no reason why they should — but the letter from the Stadhouder gained me entry, and I was invited to stand near a fire and dry off in one of the upstairs chambers. The Stadhouder suffered from asthma and was affected by cold air, so he kept fires blazing, to the discomfort of some of us.

In the circumstances I was not displeased to have to wait a while, and this was reinforced by the ready provision of wine and ham to restore me after the journey. Bouwman, the Stadhouder's personal secretary, whom I had met before, came to greet me and apologise for the delay. It seemed that William III was in conference with one of his ambassadors who had been recalled for some discussions. I suppose my four hour walk paled by comparison with his journey, so I contented myself with eating, drinking and enjoying the paintings that surrounded me, any one of which would probably have cost my whole year's earnings; except, of course, that William probably had not paid for many of them since their artists, members of a peculiarly sycophantic profession, may well have given them gratis in the hope that visitors to these large buildings would admire them and offer further valuable commissions.

This was a hard time for painters in our country. The heady prices that had preceded the French invasion had evaporated, and even as fine a master as Vermeer had died penniless. In fact, he owed his baker for a couple of years' bread, which just shows which is the more lucrative profession; and in hard times you can eat the bread you have made, but you cannot easily chew a painting.

It is just possible that after a long walk, two or three glasses of fine claret and a rest by a warm fire, I may have nodded off. In any event, I felt someone shaking my shoulder and jerked upright to see the Stadhouder walking towards me. He seemed amused rather than cross at my failure to bow, which I dashed to put right, and greeted me like an old friend. I had worked for him before, but I would not have presumed to call him an intimate acquaintance, although it seemed that he had remembered me.

'Master Mercurius! Are you well?' he asked. William was a small man, and his asthma had left him with a deformed chest rather like a pigeon, but he demonstrated his vigour by quick movement and a louder voice than was strictly necessary.

'Very well, thank you, Stadhouder. I trust that you are too.'

'Apart from occasionally not being able to breathe, I am, thank you. I'm grateful to you for coming so promptly to The Hague. I shan't beat about the bush, Mercurius. I've got a little job for you.'

Since the last "little job" the Stadhouder gave me nearly got me killed, the alert reader will understand my immediate feeling that someone had just kicked me in the groin several times.

'I'm getting married, Mercurius!'

'Congratulations, Stadhouder. May I ask who the lucky lady is?'

'I haven't decided yet. But I'm nearly twenty-six and I ought to find a bride, especially if I can enhance the security of these United Provinces by wedding a princess from one of the great powers.'

Obviously love was not a prerequisite, then.

'I look at the last war, Mercurius, and think that it could all start again at any time. But if just one of the great powers had been allied to us, would the others have dared to attack?'

Writing now it seems hardly credible that in 1672 France, England, Sweden and a few Germans formed an alliance to attack us, and eventually we fought them off under the Stadhouder's leadership. But we could hardly expect to do so again.

'The obvious choices would be princesses of France or England. Unfortunately, the King of France's daughters have all died, but he has two nieces, Marie Louise and Anne Marie. Anne Marie is only seven years old, but she would do at a pinch. Marie Louise is fifteen. I've seen a picture of her, Mercurius. She's not repulsive.'

'I am delighted to hear it, Stadhouder.'

'My bigger concern is that I know Louis XIV. He's the most self-centred man around, and if he took it into his head to attack us the fact that his niece was a hostage wouldn't give him a moment's pause. That rather defeats the object of marrying her. And, of course, she's a Catholic and the people of this country are determined that they don't want a Catholic leader. So if we had children I'd have to fight to bring them up as Protestants, and that would probably mean separating them from their mother's influence and sending her to a nunnery.'

'I can see the difficulty,' I ventured uncertainly.

'Whereas the King of England is a different matter!' William began brightly. 'He's my uncle, for a start, and we've known each other a long time.'

This was true. Charles II had been exiled in the Netherlands and lived in Breda for a while, and when he was younger William had been a guest at the restored King's court. The small problem here was that Charles had tried to introduce him to wine, women and the theatre, whereas William was much more interested in war, study and prayer. It was reported that the English King had referred to his nephew as the most boring youth in Christendom, though I don't suppose that would have stopped him marrying his daughter to William if there was any advantage in it for him.

'The snag is that Charles doesn't have any daughters,' continued William. 'Not by the Queen, at any rate. But his brother, my uncle James, has two very fine girls, Mary and Anne. Do you know anything about horses, Mercurius?'

'Only that one end has teeth and the other doesn't.'

'Well, if you breed horses you try to ensure that good characteristics are passed down and bad ones aren't. I never met my grandfather Charles I, but he was a little fellow, and when he married Henrietta Maria it was remarked that he had managed to find the only princess in Europe who was even shorter than he was. And yet my uncles are both above two yards tall, and the Princess Mary is a strapping girl. People tell me she is well above middle height. How do you account for that, then? I mean, if they were horses you'd suppose that a stray stallion got into the field.'

'It reminds us, Stadhouder, that our science is not as secure as we would like to think it is,' I suggested.

'What? Oh, you mean that we don't know what we think we know. Well, that's true, I suppose. Anyway, James has converted to Catholicism and he would like his daughters to marry French royalty, but Charles is determined that they have to remain Protestant. I'm telling you all this so you understand the background to your task, you see.'

Since no particular task had been outlined, I couldn't really say I knew what it was all about, but I nodded politely, because that seemed to be expected of me.

'The thing is, I've had a message conveyed by the Ambassador. Not our Ambassador, the English Ambassador here, Sir William Temple. Charles' chief minister, the Earl of Danby, wants us to know that he is working towards an Anglo-Dutch wedding and he thinks that the time is right to make an approach. He can't instruct their Ambassador here to start the matter without upsetting Uncle Charles, who likes to think that he is the embodiment of the government, but if we were to raise it with him, he would be bound to give the union some thought. And since, despite the advice of one or two of his ministers who want a French wedding, Charles is wary of France, we would be likely to succeed.'

'I see,' I said, because up to this point, I did.

'Danby thinks that Charles approves of me and wants to ensure that his kingdom doesn't revert to Catholicism, which would cause another civil war so soon after the last one, so marrying the second in line to the throne to me would be a guarantee of that. And if Charles told his brother that was what was going to happen, James would be bound to agree because he always does what his big brother says. In any case, the family line has always been that the King is appointed by God, meaning the King's word is law, so if James defied the King now he could hardly expect obedience when he takes the throne, as he surely will, since the present Queen of England is past child bearing. I think Danby is right about that. But I know my uncle James. He may say yes, but if the opportunity arises to jam the cogs he'll take it. And that's where you can render me a great service.'

'Stadhouder? Please explain.'

'Haven't I done so? I'm sending the Heer Van Langenburg to London as an Ambassador Extraordinary. He'll do all the normal diplomatic stuff. But I want you to go with him. Ostensibly you'll be there to ensure that the Princess Mary is a sound Protestant, but what I really want you to do is to look out for anyone who may be plotting against the marriage so it can be nipped in the bud.'

'You want me to bribe them, Stadhouder?'

'Goodness me, no! That's what we have an Ambassador for. No, just tell him what you discover and he'll deal with it. But a normal diplomat couldn't just wander wherever he wanted and speak to anyone who crossed his path whereas you, as an ordained minister there for religious reasons, can do whatever you want without embarrassing either government.'

I liked this less and less, and I thought I had a convincing argument why I was not the man for this "little job".

'Forgive me, Stadhouder, but I assume the Princess Mary doesn't speak Dutch, so how will I question her?'

'I've thought of that, Mercurius. Bouwman here speaks English, don't you, Bouwman?'

'Yes, Excellency,' came the reply, slightly guarded, I thought, as if he had no idea what was about to be suggested.

'Good. Teach Mercurius to speak English. You've got a month before you leave.'

CHAPTER THREE

There are people who will tell you that if you just speak Dutch slowly and loudly, the intelligent Englishman will understand you. That may be true, but we cannot rely on always having an intelligent Englishman to hand, and I recalled that when I questioned some English people in Utrecht on my last little job for the Stadhouder I understood not a word they said in their barbaric language. Nevertheless, I thought, if I can master Latin and Greek, I can surely pick up some English. Actually, although I did not know it then, Mary was a bit of a bluestocking and we could have conversed in Latin quite successfully. However, I could hardly rely on plotters speaking Latin when I was overhearing them, so I completely understood the need to get on top of this language.

Bouwman was very patient. We started each morning as soon as we met and continued late into the evening. I was given plays by Shakespeare to read aloud so I could get used to the sounds, and each Sunday I was sent to the British Church to hear the service and the sermon. As to the service, I understood little, and the sermon itself was near impenetrable. Dr Bowie, the minister there, was very kind to me, and made me a copy of his sermon so that I might study it at leisure, but since he spoke *extempore* his notes were sketchy, and it came to me that I could not expect people in England to write down everything they said.

My mind was somewhat eased when I was introduced to the Heer Van Langenburg.

'You're the minister who is coming with us,' he said cheerfully. 'I'm glad of that. Religion is not my forte, you understand.'

Van Langenburg was one of those irritating people who speaks four languages, plays every musical instrument known to man, and can improvise Greek quatrains at a moment's notice. In his youth he was a noted tennis player, at least until he ran at full speed into the court's wall, which accounted for his broken nose.

I had worried that my actual mission would not have been explained to him, but he soon put my concerns aside. He had been fully briefed. Thus reassured, I felt able to confess that I was finding English quite difficult.

'Don't worry,' he said. 'The English are an odd people, but one of their endearing habits is that they are always happy to talk, so you won't have to say much. Just ask them their opinion on the weather and all will be well.'

'The weather?'

'Yes, the English are fascinated about weather. They can talk about it for hours. And they are so certain that everyone in the world speaks English that even if you obviously don't, they will behave as if you do and just talk a little louder to you.'

'Have you any other advice for me?'

'Yes. Take your warmest clothes. And lots of them.'

A carriage duly arrived at the University to take me to Scheveningen, where our ship would be waiting. It was not as luxurious as other carriages I had been lent by the Stadhouder, but it had plenty of space for my trunk, in which I had stowed almost every item of clothing I owned.

The sandy shelf at Scheveningen meant that the ship had to stand off to sea and we were rowed out to it. I was in the last but one boat. It seemed that this embassy consisted of fifteen people, though I had no idea what most of them were there for, and I was no wiser after we had all been introduced.

Van Langenburg was there, and a man I took to be his personal attendant, and Bouwman had been attached to the party, presumably in case my hard-won English failed me. There was an elderly man called Preuveneers who had been included because he had known the King when he was in exile and it was hoped that Charles would be especially happy to see him again. As for the rest, I would have to learn their roles as we went along.

Bouwman, Preuveneers and our baggage filled the boat. I am not a terrible sailor, but I confess that I did not enjoy the short trip out to the ship. For some reason, the idea weighed upon me that the boat would overturn and all my possessions would descend to the depths. A little thought would have told me that the very reason why we were having to use a boat was that the sea was too shallow for a ship and the chances were that if anything fell overboard one of the swimmers amongst us could have easily retrieved it.

"Swimmers", incidentally, does not really include me. My late brother Laurentius was very happy diving into ponds or canals as a boy, and subsequently went to sea, where he died. Admittedly the proximate cause was an English bullet at the Battle of Lowestoft, but if he had kept clear of the oceans that would not have happened.

The ship's master told us to expect a two-day voyage, though he cheerfully added that if the winds were contrary it might well take double that time, or more. Wishing to reassure myself, I asked whether he had sailed to London before.

'Aye, Master,' he said, 'some years ago. But this will be an easier trip, because this time they won't shoot at us.'

'Shoot at us?'

'It was during the late war, and a merry time it was for us as we wrecked their ships. I do not propose to do that this time.'

I assured him that I was pleased to hear this and privately hoped that they did not recognise him as we docked.

We had been sent in one of William's grandest ships so that we could make some display as we arrived, but I pitied the poor mariners sent aloft to tie orange streamers to the mast, not least because it was raining. While this was unfortunate for the sailors, it gave the Lord Mayor of London something to talk about when we disembarked.

About a decade before, London had suffered an enormous fire, and rebuilding was still in hand, but my first impressions were very favourable. With much of the medieval city having gone, there was less wood and more stone than many Dutch cities could boast at that time. The carts bringing bricks from the works outside the city rolled back and forth without rest.

In the rebuilding the opportunity had been taken to widen some of the streets and reduce the overcrowding at the centre by expanding, mainly to the north. Unlike the Amsterdammers, who enlarge their city by draining the surrounding sea, the Londoners build outwards until their feverish construction absorbs the nearby villages. I was told that hamlets which were once out of town were now mere suburbs of the city. Since much of this expansion was taking place on farming land, I wondered how it would be possible to feed so great a population, who must undoubtedly someday succumb to famine and die in large numbers.

I was assured by one of the Englishmen that the city contained no less than half a million souls, and by another that there were very near two hundred thousand; at which a man called Pepys standing nearby sniffed, and said that like most enumerations, the number discovered depended upon the purpose, it being his experience that when the people were counted for taxation there were far fewer of them than when some benefit was on offer.

This Mr Pepys was the Master of Trinity House, it seems, and therefore responsible for all the lighthouses around England and Wales, not to mention the "improvement of mariners". To judge by the English sailors I had met, there remained a considerable amount of work to do in that regard.

The Lord Mayor had commenced a speech of welcome. Since we were not Englishmen, he spoke slowly and loudly, but in English, while Bouwman translated quietly for our benefit.

His name was Sir Thomas Davies, and he was a stationer, which was useful to know because I had not brought much paper with me. It was a little vexing to be uprooted from Leiden just at that moment, because I was about two-thirds of the way through writing a book evaluating the orthodoxy or otherwise of the writings of John Scottus Eriugena, and being separated from the original sources (and my paper) was extremely inconvenient. I realise, of course, that there are lecturers at universities who take the view that reading a man's work before commenting on it is an unnecessary step that merely slows the whole process down, but I felt I owed it to Eriugena to at least skim his writings before declaring that he was lucky to escape burning at the stake.

Thus distracted, I was cogitating over Eriugena's treatise *De divina praedestinatione* when I realised that Sir Thomas had stopped speaking. His delivery was so ponderous that it was a few moments before the audience realised that he intended to say no more, but the Heer Van Langenburg sprang to his feet and led us in lengthy and completely undeserved applause for the speech of welcome.

I was just looking for the exit when Van Langenburg himself began to address those present, calling Bouwman forward to translate his Dutch into English. He gave a pretty speech, neatly glossing over the repeated wars between our two countries and reminding those present of the ready welcome that King Charles had received when he went into exile in our country.

I could not resist glancing upwards to assure myself that if the heavens opened and a celestial thunderbolt issued forth in response to this perversion of the truth, I might have a moment or two to save myself. Charles was accepted largely because he was suspicious of the French, which has always been a strong point in a man's favour in the Low Countries, and when the time came for him to return to England he left a number of large debts, some impoverished hosts and, I dare say, a few bastards behind him. But the Heer skipped over all that, and merely said that he was optimistic that our negotiations would be fruitful as, in time, would be the match between William and Mary.

It seemed to me that we had been upwards of an hour listening to speeches, but when we left the quayside I could see that barely half that time had passed. I was just wondering what had next been arranged to delight us when my sleeve was plucked from behind and I turned to find myself looking at a clergyman; and, to judge by his dress, a very exalted one.

'You will forgive my introducing myself in this way,' he began. 'My name is Compton — Henry Compton — and I am delighted to see that the Prince of Orange has included a godly minister within his embassy.'

I started to look around when it dawned on me that he meant me. 'You are too kind, sir,' I replied.

'Would you prefer that we conversed in Latin?' he asked solicitously, which led me to suppose that Bouwman had been overly kind in praising my English.

'That might be a good idea,' I replied, and we adopted the old tongue.

'If your time permits,' Compton said, 'I should be greatly favoured if you would dine with me. I should be very pleased to hear something of the state of the church in your land. I understand that your Prince is very tolerant of Catholics. I will not hide my view that this may be a grave mistake, sir, but I fear that my own country may be taking faltering steps along the same treacherous path.'

The alert reader will recall that I confessed earlier to being a Catholic priest, so you may imagine that this turn of the discourse between us left me in some discomfort, but I judged it best not to cross this man, whoever he was. If he had been invited to greet us, he was plainly a man of standing.

It was true that William had pursued a policy of religious toleration. This may have been because he was wise, but I suspect that it had more to do with his unwillingness to lose the support of anyone. Thus Catholics in my land could worship in their own churches provided they were discreet, resorted there only for the Mass and accepted that many positions were closed to them as a result of their religion. During my life I held a number of posts that would have been stripped from me had my allegiance slipped out, not least of them my position at the University, which was very much a Reformed institution.

Compton was, I thought, only a few years older than I was, a well-built man with long light brown hair and a prominent nose. Not, of course, quite as prominent as the Stadhouder's; though I would never have mentioned that in front of him, since William was very touchy on the subject of large noses.

I was happy to accept Compton's invitation and promised to let him know when I had a free evening, and bowed politely as he excused himself to rejoin his party.

Van Langenburg appeared at my side. 'That's interesting,' he said. 'And what did the Bishop of London want?'

CHAPTER FOUR

I am not a man for ceremony, which may seem odd in a Catholic priest, but I mean the kind of evening to which we were now subjected.

We were conducted to our lodgings within a palace called Whitehall. We were told the King was somewhere within, but it took very little time to realise that any unplanned encounter would be very unlikely. To begin with, I never saw a grand building so badly designed. I have no doubt that at one time Whitehall was fairly proportioned and graceful, but repeated building of new walls, new windows, extensions and staircases had left it looking like it had been devised by rabbits. I left my room in search of the privy and took twenty-five minutes to find my way back, which I could not have done without the help of a passing footman.

As to my chamber, it was comfortable, and I would not have minded living there. It was not as extensive as my Leiden rooms, and there was no desk at which to work, but in compensation it was very warm and the bed was soft and well-furnished with fine curtains fringed in gold. Lest this be thought extravagant, allow me to add that they were gold in colour only, being of dyed wool, but the effect was very fine.

The itinerary prepared for us stated that we were to be conducted into the presence of His Majesty King Charles at five o'clock, after which the majority of the party would retire to enjoy a meal in one of the galleries while the King, his brother the Duke of York, and a select group of close advisers were to have a more intimate meal with the Heer Van Langenburg and a small number of his party at which some of the arrangements would be confirmed or amended. Since this meant that dinner was only a couple of hours away, I was surprised when a servant brought me a platter of meat and bread and a small barrel of wine.

'I'll return for the empty in the morning, sir,' he told me. If this was what went on throughout the palace, it was no wonder that the affairs of England were so chaotically handled, for much of the government must have been in the hands of sots.

One of the great advantages of being a man of the cloth is that I never have to spend time debating what to wear on any occasion, since my black robe will always serve; indeed, if I showed up wearing anything else I should invite comment. I therefore took out a clean black gown and fixed the other on a peg to brush it, which I was doing when I was interrupted by a pretty maid who curtseyed.

'I would do that for you, sir,' she said, 'or any other laundry that you might have.'

'Thank you,' I said. 'I'm used to doing it myself. What is your name?'

'Why, sir, I'm Meg,' she answered. 'I am to serve you and the other young gentleman.'

'The other gentleman?'

'Him with the orange rosette on his hat, sir.'

This was a fellow by the name of Constantijn Wevers, to whom I had not long been introduced myself. I was not at all sure what mijnheer Wevers' role in the party was, for I took him for some type of military man. He was silent and solitary, but I had noticed him gazing about himself during the welcome as if committing the docks to memory.

'Mijnheer Wevers?' I said.

'If that's him with the fine yellow hair, sir,' said Meg. 'I hope if you have need of a girl for any purpose during your stay you'll think of me.'

Now, I was not as versed in the ways of the world as many of my age, but young Meg left me in no doubt of the kind of need she was willing to meet. I did not propose to make use of these services and, to be frank, was more than a little surprised to find the suggestion made to a clergyman, but perhaps the Church of England is more liberal than I had been led to suppose. There were several reasons why I should refuse Meg's offer. These included very limited funds, a disinclination to avoidable sin, and a strong suspicion that women who were so free with their favours were likely to be poxed to the very armpits, and a clergyman who finds himself suffering from the distempers of Venus has some awkward explaining to do.

On the other hand, it seemed impolite to say this to her face, so I thanked her for her offer and said that I expected to be very busy.

As things turned out, I was going to be busier than I could have imagined.

I left my room at the appointed hour and found Van Langenburg in the corridor outside.

'Where's your hat, man?' he barked.

'Hat? Are we going out?'

He sighed a deep, exasperated sigh. 'You are one of those who will sup with the King tonight. You'll need a hat.'

'Surely even the English do not wear a hat in the presence of their King,' I replied.

Van Langenburg sighed again. 'No, but he'll expect you to take it off as you bow to him. And you can't take it off if you don't have it on. So, don't argue and get a hat!'

I rummaged in my trunk for something suitable. In the normal run of things, I wear a small black cap, changing to a larger square cap when I am preaching. However, I had not brought that with me, and the only other hat I had was a broad brimmed hat designed to keep the rain from my face. Reasoning that I should appear ridiculous meeting the King wearing such an everyday garment, I decided to wear my small cap and carry the large one, completing my bow with it in my hand. The King would not expect a minister to remove his skullcap, I was sure.

The discovery that I was one of the small number who would dine with the King had taken me so much by surprise that I had completely forgotten to ask why, nor did I have the opportunity to do so as the Heer Van Langenburg led our party through twisting corridors and up and down small flights of stairs in pursuit of a palace official.

We were greeted at the final staircase by the Lord Chamberlain, Lord Arlington, a fussy and pompous man who wore a patch over his nose to disguise a large scar earned in battle. I had been told something about Arlington during the voyage across, because there existed some jealousy between him and Sir William Temple.

Arlington had been sent to The Hague less than two years earlier on exactly the same mission as we were now undertaking, to procure the marriage of William and Mary, but had failed dismally. I could immediately see why that might have been, for William was a straightforward man who preferred plain speaking, and Arlington was a born schemer who had inserted one or two clauses of his own devising into the draft treaty, chiefly that William should disclose the names of any Englishman known to be disaffected to the King and should secretly co-operate in entrapping them; to which, if Van

Langenburg were to be believed, William had replied that it was beneath the dignity of any King to proceed secretly in so dishonourable a manner, so that he could not believe that his uncle Charles should desire it of him.

If William genuinely thought that, he was a bigger fool than I thought, but I suspect it was just a ruse to avoid discussions, for when Arlington raised the question of a marriage with the Princess Mary, William replied that he was not yet in a position to keep a wife as he would wish, causing Arlington to return home with his tail firmly between his legs. In fact, Van Langenburg suspected that if anyone wished his embassy to fail, it would be Arlington.

On the other hand, Arlington was keen to avoid any entanglement with France, against the wishes of some of Charles' circle who favoured such an alliance very much. Although they had been relegated to the fringes in recent months, largely because being an ally of France had proved ruinously expensive over the past few years, there were some — chiefly aligned behind the King's brother, the Duke of York — who still pursued a marriage between Mary and some leading Frenchman, the difficulty here being the short list of available candidates.

King Louis, while willing to bed anything that wore a skirt, was already married, and his brother, the Duke of Orleans, was a notorious sodomite who was one of the few in skirts whom Louis left alone. The Dauphin was already engaged to be married, and while the Duke of Orleans had a son, Philippe, he was not yet three years old. This circumstance did not seem to deter the French party in the least. I have attended very few marriages, but I think I should be uncomfortable in presiding at one where the groom cannot reach above the bride's knee.

King Louis had a substantial number of royal bastards whom he was keen to marry off, ideally to rich heiresses, but the problem here was that Charles thought it beneath his dignity to marry his daughter to an illegitimate man, and Louis thought it beneath his to accept a daughter-in-law as poor as Mary would be. This was an undoubted difficulty for the French party, but they might well try to break off any Dutch matchmaking in order to buy some time for a suitable Frenchman to appear.

Arlington was making a little speech of welcome of his own. Being an English diplomat he was, of course, speaking French, so many there had no idea what he said. This, it seemed to Van Langenburg, was a deliberate slight, because Arlington could speak Dutch tolerably well, being married to a Dutchwoman. In fact, his wife's grandfather and William's grandfather were brothers, but don't ask me to tell you what relation they were to each other, because all this "once removed" stuff gets me in knots.

Anyway, after a while Arlington concluded his welcome, and Van Langenburg replied (in Dutch), expressing our delight at being there and our regret that Arlington did not, apparently, speak Dutch, since this must deprive him of the pleasure of conversing with his wife in her native tongue. Arlington looked like he had swallowed a beggar's spittle, but interestingly he did so before the translator told him in English what Van Langenburg had said, which rather made a point, I thought.

We were conducted into the King's presence. This was a source of great anxiety to me, because I had no idea what Charles looked like and I feared that I might make my obeisance to the wrong man. As it happened, there was a tall chap with an enormous black wig sitting on a gold throne on a dais at the end of a long crimson carpet, which was a pretty good hint that he might be the King.

Each of us was introduced in turn by Van Langenburg, and then Charles said a few words. Having lived in the Low Countries for some years, Charles could manage a pretty speech in Dutch, though he must have learned it by heart because I never heard him speak the language again.

At last we were invited to sit at table and shown to our places. The Bishop of London said Grace, and once the King had picked up his spoon we all tucked in. I have to admit that after our sea voyage I was not quite as hungry as I might have been, but I ate some bread. The English have a great love of sweet things, so there were any number of pies and pastries, many containing excellent fruit.

Out of the corner of my eye I could see mijnheer Wevers. He ate heartily, spoke little, and caused some consternation when he asked for small beer rather than the jugs from which the rest of us were drinking.

'You don't like our beer?' said a big, bluff Englishman opposite him.

'No, sir,' said Wevers, 'I don't like anyone's beer.'

'Wine, then?'

'Forgive me, but I drink sparingly. It doesn't agree with me.'

The concept of moderation seems not to have taken hold in England, but our hosts appeared to assume Wevers suffered from some constitutional weakness and took no offence at his eccentricity. I wondered briefly whether the raven-haired Meg had offered herself to him yet and whether his abstemiousness ran in that direction too. I suspected it might. Wevers had the look of a man with a mission who was determined to keep his guard up until it was accomplished.

There being no ladies present that evening, the party continued well into the night and I finally flopped into bed between two and three in the morning. I was not drunk, merely desperately tired, but protocol dictated that we could not retire until the King did so, and he showed every evidence of being committed to a long drinking session until that fellow Pepys informed him that Moll Davis was returned from the theatre and waiting in his chamber, at which point Charles rose from his chair, bowed solemnly to us and raced for the door as fast as his long legs would carry him. I caught a glimpse of his younger brother James, whose face was twisted with disgust. Whatever the outward appearance, I was sure that those two lacked much fraternal feeling.

Van Langenburg suggested that the two parties should breakfast informally on the next morning — by which he really meant separately — to which our hosts were only too happy to agree.

CHAPTER FIVE

I woke early and passed a pleasant hour forgetting all about our mission, immersed in a good book. In tribute to our hosts, I had brought a copy of *Scala Perfectionis* by the Englishman Walter Hilton, who lived nearly three hundred years earlier, and was a little ruffled when I was called to set it aside and come downstairs to breakfast. It did not take me long to see that there was a heated discussion going on between Van Langenburg and a man called Vlisser. I don't think I've mentioned him before, so this may be the time to introduce him.

Vlisser was an Amsterdam merchant, somehow important in the East India Company, and reputed to be one of the richest men in our country (and therefore the world). Vlisser was no fool when it came to money, and his job was to squeeze the English for a good dowry, managing the discreet sale of anything that could be converted quickly to ready cash. William was not an avaricious man, but like many who have been brought up short of money, he was determined not to be in that position again.

Since I dislike confrontation, I paused before entering the room when I heard the raised voices. As is often the case, people who are arguing think that they have dropped their voices sufficiently to keep the dispute private, even when they can be clearly heard in the street outside. I did not deliberately eavesdrop, but I could not help overhearing the point at issue.

They were clearly talking about an Englishman to whom they had been making regular payments. Van Langenburg was arguing that they should continue this practice to ensure the success of their mission, whereas Vlisser disagreed.

'If he is going to be paid anyway, what reason does he have to conclude the matter quickly — or, indeed, at all?' Vlisser demanded.

'But if we stop the payments he may withdraw his support, and who knows whether we can bring this match about without him?'

'Surely the advantages of the marriage are self-evident. It is in his own interest to promote it.'

'But does he see that?' Van Langenburg countered.

'You're the Ambassador,' Vlisser remarked. 'You'll have to speak to him privately. Tell him there'll be no more retainers, just a lump sum when the marriage is completed.'

'I don't have the authority for that.'

'The payments are already in place, aren't they? Just tell him from now on we're holding them in trust, and he'll receive them when Mary is married to William. You don't need any permission for that.'

Van Langenburg did not reply, so I took that as my cue to enter and bid them a cheery good morning. I received two grunts in answer.

I sat at the table and helped myself to some warm bread and small beer. I suppose it was none of my business, but I could not help wondering about whom they had been speaking.

King Charles was allegedly fully occupied that morning, though one of the servants informed me that His Majesty and mornings did not mix well, and he usually lay abed until noon recovering from the evening before.

His brother James was up and about, but closeted with that man Pepys, discussing some pressing matter affecting the navy, of which James had previously been some kind of admiral. Although debarred now that he was a Roman Catholic, he retained a keen interest and Pepys made it his business to ensure that James was kept fully informed on naval matters. Prince Rupert, the King's cousin, was now head of the navy, but since he had been heavily involved in the recent war against us it had been deemed politic to send him on a tour of ports on the south coast which would last exactly as long as we were in London.

Having no prospect of any useful activity that morning, we determined upon making a tour of the city. Van Langenburg excused himself, saying that he had letters to write, but the rest of us strolled out of Whitehall Palace and went to gawp at the buildings there.

It would be churlish not to admit that London is a very fair city; and even then, with much of the rebuilding not yet completed, there were some remarkable edifices and some particularly fine churches. These were, of course, wasted upon the English, who are an irreligious people, but we paused to marvel at the Cathedral of St Paul, which will be a grand and elegant affair, if it is ever finished. We met Sir Christopher Wren, who is charged with the construction of it, who told us that it will eventually require upwards of a million pounds for its completion. For a moment I thought Vlisser was about to offer to do the work at a cut rate, but he held his peace.

We left the Cathedral to return to Whitehall for our dinner, and were walking along Fleet Street when there was a sudden rumpus. There were some stalls along the side of the road, and we had separated into smaller groups to look at the wares on sale. My eye was drawn to a bookseller's, and I was about to propose a diversion when two men grabbed Preuveneers and cried out that he was a thief, demanding that someone send for the watch. The old man appeared dumbfounded and protested volubly in Dutch that he had done nothing and was being molested without cause, but the men refused to let him go until the watch had him in charge.

In a few minutes, a sergeant and two constables arrived and appeared intent on taking him before the magistrates without delay, while the stallkeeper demanded that the thief's hand should be cut off. Judging by Preuveneers' reaction, he must have had a better knowledge of English than I had given him credit for.

Now, I will confess that I had done nothing to assist him at this point, largely because I could not think of anything useful to do, but Wevers took command, calling Bouwman to him to translate.

'If this man is a thief,' he said, 'where is your proof? What has he stolen?'

'He is a thieving foreigner,' the stallkeeper explained, with rather more emphasis on the noun than on the adjective.

'But what do you say he has stolen?' Wevers persisted.

'One of my pieces of silverwork.'

'Which one?'

'How should I know? I saw him take something from the front of the stall and slip it under his coat.'

Wevers turned his attention to the sergeant. 'Mijnheer Preuveneers will make no objection to being searched, if it is done decently and in good order.'

The sergeant motioned his men forward and they duly stripped Preuveneers to his shirt and hose, patting him down to check for hidden jewellery and carefully examining all his clothes, but they found nothing there.

'It's not here,' the sergeant concluded.

'Nor should it be,' Wevers continued, 'for I never saw him reach out to the board. Mijnheer Preuveneers is an honest man and has been falsely, perhaps even maliciously, accused, as I shall make a point of saying to the King when we meet him this afternoon.'

This was a fine bluff since no such meeting was planned, but it produced a marked effect on the sergeant, who cogitated for the briefest moment before ordering the constables to take the accuser in hand and drag him to the common jail where he would be severely questioned after so foully abusing the King's guests. I did not know what "severely questioned" meant, but it was clear that the stallkeeper did, because he began to whimper piteously and shouted that anyone could make an honest mistake.

'Aye,' agreed the sergeant, 'but this one may cost you your tongue if you're found to have borne false witness.'

As the man was led away, the bystanders respectfully opened a path for us as if urging us to leave their street as quickly as possible, so Wevers led us through and we marched briskly on.

After a while, I was able to catch up with him to commend him on his masterful display and see if I could find out any more about him by subtle questioning, but I may as well have tried to question an oyster. 'It is very lucky for mijnheer Preuveneers that you were vigilant,' I said.

'You don't know the half of it,' Wevers smiled, and opened his hand to reveal a small silver chain.

'You stole it!' I gasped.

'Certainly not!' Wevers replied. 'But neither did Preuveneers. I saw that rough fellow in the russet-coloured jerkin bump into the old man. At first I thought he was a pickpocket or cutpurse, but then I saw something bright dropped into

Preuveneers' pouch. I made it my business to remove it just as quickly.'

'So they conspired to accuse him, believing that the chain would be found in his possession? But why?'

'Presumably because we are Dutch. But it would not surprise me if this was some ruse to discredit our mission, so be on your guard, Master Mercurius. They failed today, but they may not next time.'

'I cannot help but feel some pity for the silversmith. It sounds as if his punishment may be severe.'

'I doubt they'll carry it out. But it will be instructive to see if anyone intervenes on his behalf. If they do, we'll know who is behind this.'

King Charles was furious. His face became so red I thought he might have an apoplectic seizure and drop down dead. 'Accused Preuveneers of theft!'

'I am afraid so, Your Majesty,' Van Langenburg said. 'I was not there personally, but I have been informed of the event.'

Charles rose from his seat and surveyed us all. 'Who saw this?'

Wevers stepped forward and calmly described what had occurred, omitting any mention of his own role in the matter.

Charles became incandescent with rage. 'Mr Preuveneers has been known to us since our youth. We have no doubt as to his honesty, and it pricks our honour that any of our subjects should defile his reputation in this way. Where is the silversmith now?'

'In the charge of the sergeant of the watch,' Wevers answered.

Charles turned to Arlington. 'Have him committed to the pillory today and tomorrow. That should teach him some manners.'

Arlington bowed his head in acknowledgement of the instruction. If anyone present was going to speak up for the silversmith to save him from his fate, this was their moment; but there was no plea for him.

'Preuveneers!' Charles called, and the old man came forward and knelt before the King. 'Come, come!' cried Charles, and lifted Preuveneers to his feet. 'I am heartily sorry that you have been used in such a fashion.'

It did not escape my notice that Charles was not speaking of himself as "We" any longer, but addressing Preuveneers in a more intimate and friendly tone. After the shock of the day such affection was too much for our companion, and he began to cry, apologising between sobs for his unmanliness.

'We have known each other these many years,' Charles answered gently, 'and you could never appear unmanly to me. But, by God, I will find what the villain was about! Arlington, bid his keepers do whatever they must to discover this wickedness.'

I have no taste for earthly punishments. It has long seemed to me that since we will all be judged in time by an infallible and all-knowing judge whose sentences are more awful than anything we can issue here, it makes little difference how severe we are to men on earth, and I will allow that I am perhaps a little squeamish about the shedding of blood (particularly my own). Thus, I found myself shivering at the thought of what "whatever they must" may portend. If Wevers was right, the stallkeeper was incited to this deed by others. He would pay the price, and they would escape, unless he chose to disclose their names; and who can doubt that if the tortures were severe enough, he would come up with some names, true or not? I know I would.

I was spared the extended and alcoholic dinner that afternoon because I received an invitation to meet the Princess herself. I assumed she would be somewhere in the same palace, but I was disabused of this idea as I was conducted to a carriage for the short journey to St James' Palace.

In the light of the events earlier, I was concerned to find that I was the only occupant of the carriage and might have feared a kidnapping were it not that the door bore the arms of someone ecclesiastical. Of course, I was a young man then, and the idea that clergymen might be no more trustworthy than any other man had not yet gripped me; so I took my seat, but the carriage did not move.

After a couple of minutes I was beginning to wonder whether I should jump out while I still might, when someone rushed to open the door again and the Bishop of London clambered inside.

'I am sorry I was not here to greet you, Master,' he said smoothly. 'I thought I had time to transact a little business while my servant searched you out, but I was detained by one whose invitation I could hardly refuse.'

I must have looked puzzled, because he felt the need to expand his comments.

'I mean the King, sir. His Majesty noticed my arrival.' Compton smoothed his robe and picked at an imaginary piece of fluff on his lap. 'I understand you were subjected to some unpleasantness earlier. I am sorry for it.'

'You are very kind, but you need not apologise for something in which the fault was not yours.'

'Nevertheless, we did not protect you from it.' He glanced out of the window and lowered his voice. 'I fear those who oppose this match are more resourceful than we had supposed, sir.'

'Do you think another attempt will be made?'

'I am sure of it. The names of the French party are known to us all, but we cannot be certain who is the main actor, the driving force.'

'I am told Lord Arlington has no love of us,' I suggested.

Compton smiled a thin, humourless smile. 'Lord Arlington is in favour of the match, but opposed to anyone but Lord Arlington arranging it.'

'If not him, then who?'

Compton pondered a moment. 'It might be the Duke of Buckingham.'

'I have not seen him.'

'He is currently not in favour at court. The man is appallingly immoral, openly keeping a mistress in his house while his wife was there, fighting duels and treating with the French. I do not doubt that he might bribe an official or two to be kept apprised of what is going on. And he is no lover of your country, though he once made suit to the Princess of Orange.'

'The Stadhouder's mother?'

'Yes. In his defence, she was a widow at the time. And still in mourning, I believe, though that would hardly hold Buckingham back.'

I was shocked. I ought not to have been, but these unsavoury revelations of life in high circles were a complete surprise to me. I had always thought that our betters were models of decorum. Well, if not models, then at least quite discreet about their misbehaviour.

'Then there is Sir Jasper Hollyoake.'

'Have I met him?' I stammered, fearful of showing my ignorance.

'Sir Jasper would take care that you should not see him,' Compton explained. 'He is the eyes of the French ambassador, lurking in the shadows and observing all that passes so that it may be relayed to his sponsors. This seems to me to be too bold an act for Hollyoake, but perhaps those with whom he associates have some part in it.'

I was beginning to feel that threats existed on every side, only to find that Compton had not finished yet.

'Sir Toby Roade is another possibility. He has no special love for the French, but he has a hatred for the Dutch ever since he lost two sons in the war against your nation. I did not see him about the court today.'

The carriage drew up at the front of St James' Palace, and we alighted and smoothed ourselves down. Compton led the way, and in very little time we found ourselves conducted to a large, bright room where a young woman was standing looking out of the window. As we entered, she turned and walked towards us.

I had heard that Princess Mary was tall, but it was still a surprise to see a woman taller than I was. I realised after a few moments that she was wearing shoes with heels, but even so, she was a tall girl — and not yet fully grown!

Like many a tall woman, she was not graceful, her stride being too long, and when she presented her hand for kissing I thought briefly that she meant to slap us.

'Will you sit, gentlemen?' she said.

We took our places, I slightly to the fore so that Compton could discreetly murmur a translation for any English word I did not comprehend. The Princess rang a little bell and servants appeared with a pot and some small dishes in which we were served tea, this being the fashionable drink of ladies at the English court.

'Have you drunk tea before, Master?' she asked.

'No, ma'am. I have seen it once in Amsterdam.'

'It is a great favourite of my aunt Catherine's.'

It took me a little while to realise that she was speaking of the Queen, Catherine of Braganza. I learned later that the Queen favoured tea over any other drink despite — or perhaps because of — its great expense.

I sipped at the warm liquid. It was not unpleasant, though I cannot say that I would impoverish myself to buy a pound of the stuff. It is made of dried leaves brought from China which, I suppose, explains its high price.

I am not made for parlour talk and hoped that we would soon move to more comfortable matters. Fortunately, the Princess was admirably direct.

'My father tells me that you are to examine me upon my faith, sir, and I hope you will not find me lacking in zeal for the Protestant religion.'

The reader will understand that I felt ambivalent about that point, since I was a Roman Catholic myself, albeit clothed as a Reformed minister.

I asked her some questions as if she were a child at a Catechism class, and she answered well. It was obvious that she was a young woman of some accomplishments. She was not, perhaps, pretty, though she might be accounted vivacious. Her brow was high and broad, and she had dark eyes that displayed intelligence in their quick movements.

'May I ask you, ma'am, what you think are the duties of a good wife?' I asked.

It was immediately clear that she had not been schooled to answer this question, and she looked pleadingly at Compton, who merely smiled encouragingly back at her.

'Why, sir, to be her husband's dutiful support in all things; to keep his house, to bear his children, to tend to any of his wants.'

'And could you do this for Prince William, my master?'

She grasped her dress tightly in one hand as if willing herself not to say something. 'My noble cousin is a fine and serious young man, I believe. I am told I could not have a better husband.'

'But what do you think of marrying him?' I pressed.

There was an awkward silence.

'I am my father's dutiful daughter in all things,' she replied at length.

'Are you saying you are marrying him only because your father desires it?'

'What other reason does a daughter need, sir?'

I left the matter there and asked how she felt about living in my homeland.

'My place is at my husband's side, wherever he may be.'

'I must tell you plainly, ma'am, that the Dutch court is not as gay as this one.'

Her forced smile faded. Holding a small napkin to her mouth, she rose abruptly to her feet. 'Will you excuse me a moment, gentlemen?' she asked, and left the room as quickly as she could without breaking into a sprint. The door closed behind her, and in the quiet we could hear sobbing.

'Don't take it as a bad sign,' Compton told me cheerfully. 'When the Duke of York told her she might be marrying Prince William, she cried for two days without ceasing. She doesn't do that now. Well, not as much, anyway.'

'But why is the Duke agreeing to it if he knows it will make his daughter unhappy?'

'If the Duke were a private gentleman, he would not entertain it. He is very fond of his girls. When they were small, he was often to be found on his knees playing with them. But first, he is the King's obedient subject. He believes that the King is anointed by God and that therefore his every command is to be obeyed. But the Duke is not popular in this land. Too many people are suspicious of his Catholicism and think he means to overturn our Reformation. Marrying his daughter to a staunch Protestant such as your master would demonstrate that whatever his private beliefs, he does not intend the conversion of the whole country with all the turmoil and distemper that would bring. I think he has been brought to believe that his peaceful assumption of the throne when his brother dies depends on such a match.'

That might be true, but it did not seem to me to be a good reason for marrying off your daughter.

CHAPTER SIX

I will admit that I was troubled when we returned from our meeting with the Princess. Not being the father of daughters, and having no sisters, I had never given a moment's thought to their disposition in marriage, but it seemed hard to me that effectively they had little or no say in their futures. I suppose it had always been the way, and that a loving father would do his best to secure his daughter's future by marrying her well, but I had heard too many stories of women being maltreated, ignored or deprived of the comforts of life by their husbands to feel completely at ease with the idea.

When we arrived at Whitehall, I excused myself and decided to go for a walk to gather my thoughts. It was not my place, I decided, to act on behalf of the Princess, whatever natural sympathy might be excited in my breast for a young girl so distressed; and since I had the advantage of some acquaintance with the Stadhouder, I was comfortable that he was not the sort of brute who would neglect or harm a wife. However, could I in all conscience advise him to marry a girl who by all appearances was only marrying him because her father told her to do so?

There was also the matter of her youth. William was in his mid-twenties, but she was only fifteen or so. Admittedly that was the age at which William's father had married his mother, who was only nine then herself, so I doubted William would be much moved by that consideration.

I sat in the cool of a large church and thought hard for a few minutes before deciding that there was nothing here I could manage just by thinking about it, and so I took up my hat and began walking back towards our lodgings.

About two-thirds of the way there I encountered some of my countrymen heading in the opposite direction.

'Will you join us, Mercurius?' asked Bouwman.

'Where are we going?'

'To explore some more of the city. The King is entertaining another party tonight, so it's convenient if we are not around.'

'What other party?'

'You don't want to know, Mercurius. Don't worry, it's not another embassy. In fact, I think the one thing I can guarantee they won't talk about is marriage.'

I must have looked blank, because Bouwman felt the need to expand.

'He's meeting one of his mistresses.'

'Oh.'

'But His Majesty has very generously sent Mr Pepys with us with a purse of gold for our entertainment.' Bouwman indicated a very genial-looking Mr Pepys, who bowed flamboyantly in greeting. 'I believe,' Bouwman continued in a whisper, 'that Mr Pepys is very well acquainted with places of diversion, though perhaps not all suitable for a man of the cloth.'

'That I can well credit,' I responded.

The intelligence that Mr Pepys was equipped with the King's purse must have spread far and wide, because in short order we found our company enlarged by several Englishmen. Mr Dawkins worked for Pepys at Trinity House as a surveyor of lights in the Port of London, if I understood correctly, and was a lively fellow. Being young and unmarried, he knew several places of the lower sort, and some of our party chose to follow him. Mr Laurel was a tutor at a school of which Mr Pepys was a governor, and was by all appearances a devotee of the table, which seemed much more to my taste, so I adhered to his troop and together we trailed through some narrow alleys until we reached a tavern at which, according to Mr Laurel, the roast beef and mutton chops were unsurpassed. Securing a large table, we sat down and awaited our meal.

Mr Laurel had arranged that we would meet the others by nine o'clock at some particular place, and clearly intended to do an evening's dining every hour until then. Pies, platters of roast meat and bowls of turnips and carrots appeared and were emptied with regularity. I was pressed to eat and drink far more than I wanted, though I must confess that the beef was very good, and I allowed myself to be tempted to a second plate thereof. However, I needed to keep a clear head and therefore drank sparingly.

There were a couple of other Englishmen attached to us. One, by name of Buckie, turned out to be a Scot who had been part of the King's party when he was in Scotland and later in exile. Buckie talked amiably enough, though his accent was such that I had not the slightest clue what he was saying, and contented myself with agreeing with his observations whenever he paused and looked in my direction.

The other was a gallant introduced to us as Captain Hallow. If Hallow was a military man, his post must have been honorary, since he was far too concerned with his appearance ever to have faced a field of battle. He regularly checked his neckcloth in the polished platters as they were emptied, and bobbed off his seat to ensure that the loose end of his sash was not folded beneath him. Hallow had started the evening with Dawkins' party but found them, he said, rather rowdy and ungentlemanly.

While I enjoy my food, I am not a glutton and I was very glad when Laurel announced that if we were to keep our appointment for the second part of the evening we must quit the place at once. It appeared that he had secured invitations to a rout somewhere, which seemed to be some sort of party with gambling and drinking, so Laurel procured each of us a bottle of claret wine to take with us, which passed as the price of admission. I have no idea where we were going, because something happened to prevent our passage.

Mr Dawkins' party had been in company with diverse actresses and dancers from London's theatres. I think there is no need to describe what may have occurred there. Having torn themselves away from this, they were waiting at the rendezvous point where Laurel gave them each a bottle of wine to take to the rout. I was about to excuse myself and say that I would return to my room when there was a cry from Van Langenburg.

'Where's Wevers?'

It was quite dark, but as we all stepped into the light of a door-lamp it was clear that he was not with us.

'We thought he was with you,' Bouwman explained.

'No, we thought he was with you,' replied Van Langenburg.

'Then we must retrace our steps to see where he was last seen,' I suggested. In this we were rather hampered by our lack of geographical knowledge and our hosts' lack of sobriety, but Dawkins appeared to grasp the importance of our loss and it sobered him considerably.

Leading the way, he took us back towards the point at which we had divided into two groups. Although I had completely failed to notice it earlier in the evening, it was now clear that we had separated outside the church of St Martin-in-the-Fields, with my group having continued along the high road while

Dawkins' party had made for the waterside where they were more likely to meet with the kind of entertainment they wanted. The main road was busy and well lit, so we retraced Dawkins' route and just before their first stop, a tavern called The White Cat which looked out on the river, we noted a small alleyway which led to the back of the tavern. It was littered with empty barrels, general rubbish, and the body of a fair-haired man.

Wevers was lying face down on the sparsely cobbled surface. An ornate black and gold dagger protruded from his back just to the left of his spine. It looked slightly familiar, but I could not remember why.

'What are we going to do?' Laurel asked, as much to himself as to anyone in particular.

'We cannot leave him here,' answered Van Langenburg. 'We should carry him back to the Palace.'

Pepys produced the King's purse. 'Let us procure a cart of some kind,' he said, and sent Dawkins in search of one.

'Before we move him, we should examine the scene for any clues,' I announced, not in any great hope that I would find any, it being a dark alley with plenty of litter on the cobbles.

Laurel had obtained a lantern by the light of which we could see rather better.

I knelt beside the body and was surprised to hear Bouwman say, first in Dutch and then in English, 'Please give the Master some space. He has experience of investigating murders.'

'Murder?' gasped Captain Hallow.

'Well, self-evidently a man cannot drive a dagger into his own back,' Pepys responded.

'No, I … I suppose not,' Hallow agreed, though he looked as if his wits were failing him.

I remembered, somewhere in the back of my mind, what Dr De Graaf said some years earlier when he was examining the body of little Gertruyd Lievens in Delft. 'Let us not touch until we have seen,' he had said, and it was good advice. That way we can be sure that any marks on the corpse are of the killer's making, and not of ours; and so I restrained myself from touching anything until I had committed the scene to memory. I can see it still, many years after the events.

Wevers lay face down, his head turned to the right, his hat still attached but pushed back, presumably as he hit the ground. His eyes were open and there was no particular expression on his face. I had heard that when a man dies the last thing he sees is indelibly retained in his eyes, but I could see nothing except the look of sudden death.

Blood dribbled between the cobbles from under the body at his right side, and his hair fanned out over his shoulders, almost reaching the top of the blade. By the lantern I could see something I had not previously noticed; the initials AV were stamped into the handle of the dagger, and it was then that I remembered where I had seen the dagger before. It had been in a matching short scabbard hanging at the belt of Antonij Vlisser.

My nature is to be open, but I was learning that there are some things the wise man keeps to himself rather than blurting them out to all and sundry, so I said nothing about what I had seen until we were back at the Palace. Pepys had secured the use of a small chamber in the cellar where we could store Wevers' body and mount a guard to prevent any interference with it.

We crowded into the room as the porters carried Wevers in and laid him on a board upon two trestles. Lord Arlington, who had joined us, called for lights.

'This is indecorous,' Arlington pronounced. 'Can we not at least place him in a position of repose?'

'That would require us to remove the dagger,' I began.

Having thus drawn attention to the object, which could now be seen much more plainly, it did not surprise me when Captain Hallow spoke out. 'Is that not Mr Vlisser's dagger?'

Vlisser acknowledged that it was so.

'And yet you did not say so before?' Pepys asked.

'I did not see how it could be mine,' Vlisser remarked, 'because I knew my own dagger to be here in safe keeping.'

When we had arrived at the Palace, some of our company had had weapons of varying kinds upon them. These were mostly ornamental, the sort of thing our young gallants swagger about town with, but it is not the done thing to bring a weapon into the presence of the King, so we had all surrendered them. They had been returned at the end of the audience, and then re-confiscated each time the King appeared. So far as I knew, our party had all decided to leave their weapons in their trunks for the duration of the stay. It was not impossible that Vlisser had decided to wear it again before stepping out in the town, but the look on his face showed that he had not done so; or, I suppose, that he was a great actor.

Arlington screwed his face up in the manner of one who has just stepped from his front door into a fresh pile of manure. 'It grows late, and we can do nothing to help Mr Wevers. Let us lock this chamber and post guards here. We will attend to him in the morning. Meanwhile, Mr Vlisser, we should, with your permission, examine your trunk to verify that this is indeed your dagger.'

'Of course,' Vlisser mumbled.

'It would not be appropriate to imprison a member of an official delegation from a friendly nation,' Arlington declared, 'but I trust we have your word that you will not leave the Palace without the King's permission?'

I think we all knew that the guards on the gates would be told that Vlisser was not to leave, whatever international incident might arise by detaining him, but before Vlisser was able to assent, Van Langenburg intervened. 'As leader of this mission, I give my word that none of us will do so,' he said, thus neatly skirting around the question of whether any one person might be detained and reminding the English that a Dutch citizen answered to him, and not to the English King.

Much of the party dispersed, but Van Langenburg, Arlington, Pepys and I mounted the stairs to Vlisser's chamber. I had not been invited, but my curiosity was piqued and I had an idea that the Stadhouder would want me to do so.

Van Langenburg spoke up again. 'Master Mercurius has some experience of these matters in the Stadhouder's service,' he explained, 'and has brought many a criminal to justice.'

The sin of pride reared its head for a moment, before a small voice inside my head noted that unless you can define "six" as "many" I had not brought too many to account; and, to tell the whole truth, I allowed one to escape, and another died before he was tried. On the other hand, nobody here needed to know that. I was pleased to see Arlington look me up and down with a new respect — or, at least, a different kind of supercilious contempt.

'I am sure we will be pleased to have the Master's powers to support us,' Arlington replied.

I had not yet become attuned to the English way of speaking, and I was unsure whether the tone was one of rank condescension or polite disbelief. Anyway, we arrived at the room and Vlisser pushed the door open. It was not locked, because guests' rooms in palaces are generally left open for the maids to go about their business. As leader of the delegation Van Langenburg had a guard stationed outside his room. The rest of us shared a couple of soldiers who roamed the corridors to keep us safe.

Vlisser indicated his trunk, which was on the floor beneath one of the windows. It was made of wooden panels fixed to an iron frame, with a hinged lid. Two large iron bands wrapped round it, but there was no lock as such. A bar passed though loops on the lid and hasps on the face of the chest to hold it shut, and a peg could be driven in each end of the bar to secure the trunk for travel, though, of course, the pegs were not in place now.

Arlington maintained his pretence that Vlisser was a gentleman whose words and actions were not to be questioned. 'Perhaps, Mr Vlisser, you would be kind enough to show us where you put your dagger?'

It suddenly dawned on me that Arlington was speaking Dutch — of a sort — which must have perplexed Mr Pepys. I was later to discover that Mr Pepys had a little French, Italian and Spanish but was wont to mingle them in the same sentence, particularly when talking about his lady friends.

Vlisser lifted the lid of his chest, took out some gloves and shirts which were folded on top, and thus revealed the scabbard below them. As anticipated, it was empty.

'Thank you, Mr Vlisser,' Arlington said. 'Gentlemen, I think there's no more to be done tonight. Let's to our beds and meet again in the morning to recount this melancholy episode to His Majesty.'

Thus we all returned to our chambers, where I sat on the edge of the bed pondering what I had seen. There were at least four things that I thought needed some explanation; five, if you included the question as to why Vlisser would intend any harm to Wevers.

CHAPTER SEVEN

I woke in the morning with the strange feeling that there was a passage of scripture that might throw some light on this affair, though I could not recall it precisely. After a bit of searching, I found it in the seventh chapter of the book of Proverbs. *Irretivit eum multis sermonibus, et blanditiis labiorum protraxit illum. Statim eam sequitur quasi bos ductus ad victimam, et quasi agnus lasciviens, et ignorans quod ad vincula stultus trahatur: donec transfigat sagitta jecur ejus...*

It describes a man who is travelling and comes across a seductive woman. Roughly translated, it says "Her fancy words made him give way, the flattery from her lips overcame him. He chased after her like an ox going to the slaughter or a fool to punishment in the stocks: till a dart pierced his liver."

Wevers was a handsome man. Meg had confirmed that to me. Was it possible this was just an argument over some woman or other?

But Wevers had been so self-contained. If he had wanted a woman, Meg would have obliged him, I had no doubt. He might have had cause to regret it, because women who are so wickedly unchaste are often full of the pox, but then so could be any other woman he met. Besides, none of us recalled seeing him during the evening. It was likely that he had been killed very soon after we had separated, in which event he cannot have had much time to get himself into any kind of trouble. From St Martin-in-the-Fields to the lane was barely a hundred paces, five minutes' walk at most. Given the busy nature of the thoroughfare outside the church, he could not have been killed there, so he must have walked to his fate himself. But where had he been going? Was he just straggling at the back of Dawkins' party?

I was convinced that despite his carefree air, Dawkins would have been warned strictly against letting any of us get into trouble. How could he have mislaid a Dutchman and not noticed for the whole evening? Unless, of course, he did not think Wevers was ever part of his party. Had Wevers struck out on his own, in a city he did not know?

Or did he?

We gathered together for breakfast. When I say "we" I mean the Dutch party, except for Vlisser, who had no appetite. It was a sombre meal, partly out of respect for our departed comrade, but also because we all had an unvoiced suspicion that this may not be the end of our troubles.

Van Langenburg addressed us, asking that we remain circumspect in any comments we might make and encouraging us not to speculate vainly on the events of the evening before. He had, he said, no doubt of Vlisser's innocence, though he did not say what made him so sure. For myself, I had reached the same conclusion but only because I could not imagine Vlisser being able to take Wevers by surprise. I thought back to Wevers' quick action when he saw Preuveneers under attack and his general air of someone who knew how to use a sword. Admittedly he did not have a sword when he was killed, but he did not appear to have struggled either, although all I knew about him suggested that he would not give up his life easily. Vlisser was a ruthless businessman, I have no doubt, but that is a very different thing from killing a man in cold blood.

Lord Arlington had insisted that all the Englishmen present on the previous evening remained at the Palace until the King dismissed them. Buckie had objected strongly that there was no reason to suppose that any of them was the killer when it could very easily have been a mere pavement footpad, but he was firmly told the King required it. I doubt that the King knew the first thing about it at that stage, because I was fairly sure I had seen the royal carriage returning just before I came down for breakfast and decanting a sleepy occupant who was probably looking forward to a long nap in his bed.

I was quietly chomping on a piece of bread and cheese when Lord Arlington himself appeared. We respectfully began to stand, but he flapped us down impatiently and headed straight for Van Langenburg, with whom he exchanged a few words. Since these words were accompanied by the pair of them looking at me, I began to feel more than a little uneasy, and rightly so, because Van Langenburg beckoned me to come to him.

'Master Mercurius, your fame flies before you. His Majesty wishes to speak to you about the death of poor Wevers. Will you please go with Lord Arlington?'

'Gladly, mijnheer.'

Arlington began walking away and I made to follow, only to have my sleeve plucked by Van Langenburg, who hissed into my ear. 'Impress him, Mercurius. Get this right and it will grease the machinery of courtship.'

For some reason, my mind began to imagine what a machine used for courtship would look like and which bits might need greasing, then I realised it was just a figure of speech. I am altogether too literally-minded sometimes.

We weaved our way through the passages once again. At least twice I was convinced that Arlington was lost but just kept going as if to give the impression that he knew where we were, but at length we came to a corridor with a couple of armed guards outside a room. To my surprise, we walked past that door and turned in at the next, which was empty.

'I thought we might be going in that room we just passed,' I said, as much to break the silence as anything.

'Hardly,' Arlington replied. 'That is His Majesty's privy.'

'Ah. That explains the guards.'

Arlington looked at me as if I had designs to steal the King's commode. Fortunately, at that moment the door was flung open and the King entered, looking rather dishevelled in his nightshirt and a gold and black overgown. He was wearing his wig, but it was not quite straight. 'Arlington. Mercurius,' he greeted us before flopping back on his bed. 'This is a damnable business.'

'Indeed, sir,' Arlington oozed.

'There are people who don't want this wedding to go ahead, but I didn't think they'd stoop to this.'

'They are desperate men, Your Majesty.'

'I want them caught, Arlington. Then I want them hanged. We may have to have a trial of sorts in the middle, but I'm not precious about that. I will not have my plans thwarted in this way.' The King turned his attention to me. 'Forgive us, Master Mercurius,' he said. 'We are neglecting you shamefully. If your English fails, no doubt Arlington will translate. He claims not to speak Dutch, but we know otherwise. Who is the dead man?'

'Constantijn Wevers, Your Majesty,' I said.

The King's eyebrow arched as if this was a promising but ultimately inadequate identification.

'A young man with yellow hair, quite reserved,' I added.

'Oh, the spy! Yes, I noticed him.'

'Spy, Majesty?' I stuttered.

'Oh, come, Mercurius, don't say you didn't know?'

'I didn't, sir, I swear.'

The King chuckled. 'Well, I don't suppose they would tell you. Every embassy includes a spy, Mercurius. If things go badly and the two parties fall out, he can give some guidance to their armies and navies when diplomacy is being conducted by other means.'

'His Majesty means war,' Arlington explained.

'I sincerely hope it will not come to that,' I stammered.

'Don't worry, he hadn't got far. And he was being followed, wasn't he, Arlington?'

Arlington looked as if he had eaten an unripe plum.

'Come on, Arlington, out with it, man!'

'He gave our man Morley the slip at St Martin-in-the-Fields, sir.'

'More fool him. Morley might have protected him had he still been in touch. How did he get away?'

'He was not a novice, sir. He stepped into a tavern, hid behind the door until Morley entered, then slipped out behind him, we think.'

'Throw Morley in a dungeon for a couple of days to reflect upon his inadequacy, Arlington. He's a good man, but he's getting cocky.'

'I'll see to it, Your Majesty.'

'So do we know where Wevers was going?'

'He was waylaid in an alleyway when he was heading south, so I presume he was going down to the river.'

'Probably looking for signs of shipbuilding. He would know our navy isn't there.'

I recalled the way Wevers had been looking along the river when we were being greeted, as if appraising something.

'So tell me,' the King continued, 'how was Wevers found?'

'We retraced our steps to look for him and found him in a side alley. He was face down with a dagger sticking out of his back,' I explained.

'Do we know whose dagger?'

'A man called Vlisser, Your Majesty, one of our party.'

Charles tore a piece of bread and dunked it in a cup of wine before turning it over in his mouth a few times while he considered this. 'Well, I can't hang a Dutchman who is part of an official party, but no doubt if I drop young Prince William a note he'll do the decent thing and sort the matter out when you return.'

'Forgive me, Your Majesty, but I don't think Vlisser did it.'

'No? Whyever not?'

'Two reasons. First, why leave the dagger in Wevers' back for everyone to find when just a few steps away there was a great big river into which he could have thrown it? Second, the wound in Wevers' back did not bleed. If it did not bleed, that is because he was already dead when the blade was driven in. And he was dead, because I think we are going to find today that he was actually stabbed from in front. He was lying in a puddle of blood, but none had run down his coat; therefore, he was bleeding somewhere we could not see in the dark.'

Charles did a bit more dunking and chewing. 'Yes, I can see that argument. Arlington, is there to be an examination of the body?'

'Yes, sir. I have sent for your personal physician and a surgeon he has recommended.'

'Good. See that Mercurius is admitted too. We have to be seen to be making every effort to get this right. Report back to me after the examination.'

We both bowed and I began to edge backwards, only to realise that Arlington was standing his ground. This was, it seemed, his way of conveying that he had somewhat more to say, if invited to do so.

'Yes, what is it, Arlington?' asked the King testily.

'It may be opportune to arrest some members of the French party…' he began.

'Is there any evidence against them?' Charles barked.

'No, but if we question them…'

'They are not going to succeed,' Charles argued. 'Their star is declining. I have gone as far as I dare with the King of France, and they must know that the people will not tolerate any more alliances with Louis XIV.'

'You will forgive my bluntness, Your Majesty, but some of them believe that you intend to follow your brother into the Catholic church and that when he is King the alliance will be revived.'

'Jermyn is too busy laying out his great estate to return to intrigues,' Charles thundered. 'Besides, he needs the money. He can't afford to plot. Nobody will take a promissory note from him.'

Arlington held his tongue, and Charles' choler slowly subsided.

'I will speak to my brother. Unless there is clear evidence linking Jermyn and his party to this, let him be. He served me well for many years, Arlington. I will not condemn him without cause.'

As Lord Arlington and I descended to the cellar where Wevers lay, I asked him about this man Jermyn whom the King had mentioned.

'Jermyn? Earl of St Albans and my predecessor as Lord Chamberlain. Jermyn was very strongly in favour of a French alliance.' Arlington paused on the stairs as if he would say more, but dared not; then he decided to unburden himself anyway. 'Be he e'er so mighty, a subject is still a subject, Master. Jermyn forgot that. And the King is a good man, a generous man, but it is in the nature of good rulers to be ruthless. We all know that whatever has gone before, if we cause him serious discomfiture we will be discarded. I know that. You see me now at the peak of my power; tomorrow morning I may be sent back to my estate in Suffolk. If I transgress badly, I may not even have an estate in Suffolk to return to. I make no complaint about that. We who serve Kings know what our future holds, and no doubt it is the same in your land.'

I thought it politic to nod, although William was not a vindictive master.

'It is a long story,' Arlington continued, 'and my own part in it is not glorious. It was the King's will that we should ally ourselves with France. To this end, we signed the Treaty of Dover. But actually there were two Treaties, one public and one private. The private one, which I negotiated, laid more obligations upon Great Britain and the King than we thought Parliament would countenance. Anyway, as you will know, the Treaty committed us to attacking your country. What we had not anticipated was that your master would be able to wrest power into his own hands and fight back.'

This much I knew. The De Witt brothers were removed from office and lynched, and William installed himself as Stadhouder, as his father had been. Thanks to his leadership we fought the French to a standstill, stopping them just twenty miles from Amsterdam. Not only that, he sent ships to attack the English coast, which effectively forced the English out of the war.

Arlington continued. 'Parliament refused to vote more money for the war unless the King revoked the measures he had taken to ameliorate the position of Catholics and removed them from any office they held under the Crown. The French knew then that the Treaty was a dead letter, because Charles would never be able to implement it. Jermyn's stock fell, and it plummeted even more when news of the secret treaty leaked out. We have the Duke of Buckingham to thank for that. He sought to bring me down, but he misjudged the reactions of the King and Parliament. The King was deeply embarrassed by the disclosure of the secret treaty, and threw Buckingham out of the Privy Council. I am afraid that Buckingham then accused me of treason, and I feared for my neck, but His Majesty was graciously pleased to make peace with your country, as part of which we agreed to give no further aid to the French. Whatever you may think of me, Master Mercurius, I will carry out whatever happens to be the King's pleasure at the time. Jermyn and Buckingham were so closely associated with the French alliance that they were compelled to resign.

'Neither of them is wealthy, because they are both devoted to gambling. But Jermyn owned a large parcel of land near St James upon which he is building. His design is very grand; he aims to provide homes for the better sort of people in London, together with places of business and entertainment, and it may make him rich, but it has occupied all his time for some while. However, who knows if he and Buckingham have maintained connections with the French Court? They would certainly both like to see this marriage prevented.'

'Do you think they would involve themselves in such a plot?' I asked anxiously.

Arlington smiled thinly. 'Jermyn never saw a plot he didn't like.'

It was reassuring to see that Wevers was still where we had left him. The medical men had not yet arrived, so I busied myself in saying prayers over his body until they were announced. Sir Charles Scarburgh was the King's own physician, a very learned gentleman and a graduate of both Cambridge and Oxford. He was a dark-haired man in his mid-fifties, with a prominent brow indicating, no doubt, a lot of brain beneath. He had unusually long fingers which he used dexterously as he went about his work.

Unfortunately, the King's serjeant-surgeon had recently died, so in his place we were attended by Dr Nathaniel Hodges, a physician of repute who had done great service during the late plague in London. Hodges was a rather younger man, and a fervent proponent of the drinking of sack as a prophylactic against all manner of pestilence. During the great plague he had drunk several cups a day, and despite his close attendance upon the sick he had escaped infection. Now he liked to start the day with a large tumbler just in case he came across something contagious later, and it was fairly clear to me that he was playing it safe in case being stabbed with a dagger was contagious.

Introductions were effected, and we took our places, Scarburgh at the left side, Hodges to the right, and Arlington and I by the head.

'Have you attended a post-mortem examination before?' Scarburgh asked.

'I have,' I replied.

'Good. Then you know what will happen. If you feel unwell, please leave. Don't fall across the corpse. It is inconvenient and it might be dangerous.'

The doctors removed their coats and donned aprons.

'Well, now there's a curiosity, is there not?' Scarburgh remarked.

Hodges obviously thought that something was expected of him, so he replied, 'You refer to the dagger, sir?'

'Indeed. I'll warrant there's no blood when we remove it. Shall we?'

Scarburgh made no move at all, having cast Hodges as his student for the day, so the younger man placed his hand flat on Wevers' back and gently pulled on the weapon's handle until it came free. Placing it on a towel, he offered it for inspection to us all.

'That is not a dagger that has been inserted in a living man,' Scarburgh opined. 'Now, if one of you gentlemen will come to the feet, we shall turn him over.'

I gripped the ankles as instructed.

'Push them together, sir! Let them move as one. Now, upon my command — one, two, three!'

Wevers flopped inelegantly on his back, and was pulled back into position by Hodges. We could immediately see a much more serious wound in Wevers' chest which had bled profusely, the shirt being stiff with dried blood. Scarburgh teased the shirt open and laid his thumb alongside the wound.

'I assume the dagger was not used for this wound, sir?' I asked.

'Quite correct. Plainly the dagger is too clean, but in any event this wound was made by a much narrower blade. A stiletto or something of the kind, and by the look of it at least six inches long. Let us remove his clothes and we can verify my guess.'

'Before you do, may I check something?' I asked.

Somewhat surprised, but willing to indulge me, Scarburgh gestured to me to come forward. I lifted Wevers' left arm until

.

it was nearly vertical, whereupon there was a clatter as his own poniard dropped out of the large cuff and onto the floor. I retrieved it and laid it in front of Scarburgh.

'My word! How did you know that was there?'

'I didn't, but Wevers was a military man. I could not imagine he would not have a concealed weapon when he went abroad. Being right-handed, he would keep it in his left sleeve. And yet he had no opportunity to use it.'

'Indeed, death surprised him, as it will us all one day. Now, this blade is much more like the one that pierced his breast.'

'May I ask,' Hodges enquired, 'what this gentleman's profession was?'

'I have no idea,' I said.

'Come, sir, don't be coy,' said Scarburgh.

'I am not coy,' I said, not entirely sure what coy meant but divining from their tone that it was being suggested that I knew but was not telling them. 'I had not met him before this mission, and I was not told what his purpose was. In fact,' I added, to head off further impertinent questions, 'I don't know why most of the Dutch party are here.' *Including me*, I thought.

'Nevertheless,' Scarburgh insisted, 'you said he was a military man.'

'My guess,' I said. 'I do not know it to be a fact. He carried himself like a military man.'

'Well,' said Scarburgh, 'if military men step out with stilettos in their sleeves, we may surmise that a military man is just the sort of person who may have killed him.'

Yet Wevers did not appear to have defended himself at all. He plainly did not anticipate the blow that felled him, and I knew that his hands were as quick as mercury. Even someone a yard away would have been taking a risk. Was it possible that

Wevers did not expect the blow because he knew his assassin? Could it have been another member of the Dutch party?

Whoever it was, I doubted that it was Vlisser. Vlisser was no fool, and he would hardly have made a point of sticking his own monogrammed dagger in the victim's back, having previously killed him with something else, especially when the Thames was only a few dozen paces down the road. It was much more likely that the true killer was trying to throw the blame on Vlisser, but why? Was it important that it was Vlisser, or would any of us have sufficed?

The examination continued for some time, but I found no matter of particular interest to my enquiry. In due time the doctors had completed their gory work, and Scarburgh set about sewing Wevers back together again.

'He was in fine physical condition when he died,' he remarked.

'Very sturdy,' agreed Hodges.

'Thank you,' I replied. 'But he is just as dead as if he were an elderly sot.'

'We take your point, Master,' said Arlington, whose presence I had almost forgotten. 'Let us come away, and take this dagger to His Majesty, if the doctors have no objection?'

They signalled that they had none.

'Will we be allowed near him with it?' I asked anxiously.

'I think I may be,' said Arlington, 'if the blade be pointing at my own breast.'

I must have looked puzzled, because Arlington smiled.

'That was a pleasantry, Master,' he explained. 'His Majesty knows I would do him no harm. If I had wanted to do so, I have had many opportunities over the years, believe me.'

CHAPTER EIGHT

As we ascended the stairs to the palace, an idea came to me. 'May we examine Wevers' room?' I asked. 'Perhaps there is something there that might tell us where he was going.'

Arlington readily agreed. 'But I will have to find out where he was accommodated,' he added.

'It's close to my room. We shared the same maid.'

Arlington led the way, as a result of which I now knew another route to my corridor, though I very much doubted if I would ever find it again. On the way, Arlington despatched a servant to bring him a paper which described the room allocations.

The corridor had a passageway along one side, with four rooms to our right. The first, it seemed, was Bouwman's. Next to him was Preuveneers', then mine, and finally Wevers'. At that point the corridor turned to the right and then forked, with another corridor leading to the left where other members of our party were housed. Vlisser's room was the second one on that corridor. Van Langenburg was in more luxurious apartments on the floor below, I discovered.

As I expected, the doors were unlocked — in fact, they could not be locked. The first thing I observed on entering Wevers' room was that it was colder than mine. The fire had died down and the grate had not been cleaned out. His bed had not been slept in, of course, and on the end of the counterpane lay a shirt and some hose for laundering. We worked steadily around the room, looking for any notes or other evidence of an appointment.

'Surely if it ever existed he would have burned it?' suggested Arlington.

I looked in the grate, but I could see no evidence of burnt papers. 'Lord Arlington, suppose that the appointment was made verbally, and that Wevers was a stranger to your city. What landmark could he have been given as a meeting-place, easy to find, ideally one where a foreigner such as he might not be remarkable?'

'Clearly the riverside teems with foreigners. And there are any number of taverns there with simple signboards.'

'Indeed, but Wevers would have been wary about going into any low drinking place on his own. The meeting-place must have been more public.'

Arlington's face lit up. 'The Savoy!'

'What is this Savoy?' I asked.

'A hospital, with chapels and so on. It lies on the riverside, two or three hundred yards from St Martin's. It was designated as a hospital for those injured in the Dutch Wars, but it also houses chapels for non-conformists. There is, for example, a German Lutheran church within its precincts, so respectable foreigners are often to be seen there.'

'A church or chapel would be a good meeting-place. But surely there is a much shorter route from here to there along the river?'

'Yes, but you will recall that Wevers was being followed. There would be little opportunity to throw off a follower on the embankment. And he may have wanted to give the impression that he was with your party.'

It was all becoming clearer. Wevers would have an appointment, let us say at around seven o'clock, which would make sense because it was after six o'clock when I had bumped into Bouwman and joined the party. When we arrived at St

Martin's and separated into the two groups, none of us noticed Wevers slipping off to keep his appointment, and he no doubt intended to rejoin us at nine o'clock when the parties reconvened. We had no idea what the appointment could have been about, or with whom it was made, but was it likely that anyone could have slipped out, killed Wevers and come back without any of us noticing? I would have said not, were it not for the incontrovertible fact that none of us had remarked on Wevers' own absence.

Another mystery was nagging at me too. There had been a lot of blood on the cobbles, and Wevers' shirt was thick with clotted blood. It seemed unlikely that anyone who stabbed him could have avoided being splashed, and yet I noticed no traces on anyone in Laurel's dinner party. Did that mean that the killer was in the other section that had gone with Dawkins? But we had stood together in good light outside St Martin-in-the-Fields when we met again, and nobody was spotted with blood. They might, perhaps, have concealed it with a cloak, but if Wevers had died early in the evening, as seemed to be the case, they could hardly have worn the cloak all night in company.

When we found his body, Wevers had been dead for some time. He was becoming cold to the touch; and since he was found no more than three hours after we had all set off from Whitehall, that surely supported the notion that he had died nearer to seven o'clock than nine.

I explained these thoughts to Arlington, who turned them over in his brain for a while.

'Then may we conjecture,' he asked, 'that Mr Wevers was killed on his way to the appointment? Which may, therefore, be no appointment at all, but only a ruse to ensure that his whereabouts at a particular time would be known.'

There are times when I feel a complete dolt, and this was one. I had been wondering how the killer could have been at the Savoy Hospital at seven o'clock, killed Wevers, moved his body and rejoined us without being noticed, but he need never have been at the hospital. All he needed to know was that Wevers was going to be walking from St Martin's to the Savoy shortly before seven o'clock. He could even have killed Wevers on his way to join us; at the most it was five minutes' walk to Laurel's chosen tavern and even less to the White Cat.

We busied ourselves in inspecting the contents of Wevers' chest. Arlington lifted them out onto the bed and we checked each item in turn for hidden documents. When the chest was empty, Arlington sighed. 'Nothing. Absolutely nothing.'

I was surprised because there were two things I had not found. On the voyage, Wevers had been reading a small New Testament very like my own, but I could not see that anywhere. More to the point, if Wevers had been a spy, I should have expected him to have some kind of writing case so that he could make his reports. It seemed unlikely that he would take a chance on being able to borrow paper and ink wherever he went.

I knew from one of my previous enquiries that almost any bodily fluid will serve as ink, particularly if secret writing is required. Urine is readily available, and the writing will appear if the paper is heated; but that still requires paper and a nib.

'My Lord,' I said to Arlington, 'may I borrow your staff a moment?'

Arlington handed over the tall staff he carried as a token of his office. I placed one end on the floor beside the chest and marked the top of the chest with my thumb. I then repeated the measurement with the rod on the base of the chest.

'My word!' Arlington gasped. 'That is an unusually thick base to a chest. Do you suspect that there might be a secret compartment?'

I certainly did. 'It would be inconvenient if the whole contents of the chest had to be emptied any time that Wevers wanted to access it,' I offered, 'so let us suppose that it slides out.'

We dragged the chest forward so that we could see all sides. It seemed to me that the mechanism could not be too delicate because Wevers could not risk it springing open when, for example, it was being loaded aboard ship. Logic suggested that there must be two actions needed, buttons to be pressed simultaneously or some such arrangement.

The chest was of wood with a leather top held in place by brass studs. The studs themselves were evenly spaced, and the leather covered the whole top except for the hinges. We worked the lid a few times and saw nothing obvious at first, but then it came to me.

With the lid open as far as possible, you could see, just below the mid-point of the back edge of the chest proper, an iron shield. It looked like a maker's mark or some similar badge; but why put it on the inside, where nobody would see it? After a bit of experimentation, I found that it would slide upwards by a thumb's length or so, and that it appeared to be connected to some sort of rod. That iron rod locked the secret drawer and prevented its coming open accidentally. With the rod lifted, I pressed on the lower back rail of the chest and was rewarded with the sound of a spring pushing the drawer out. I carefully slid it forward, and Arlington and I looked at the contents.

There was a small handgun with a flask of powder and some lead balls, all wrapped in oilcloth. A stylus which would serve as a nib was inserted down the spine of a notebook which proved to include a list of symbols and names, and obviously served as a codebook. Arlington, for example, was BP — perhaps for Black Patch? — whereas the Duke of York was the letter E inside a circle. I was a capital letter L with a crossbar through the stem, converting it to a cross — a holy man from Leiden? — but the most interesting thing we saw was a letter written in Dutch.

It commanded Wevers to deliver the "encouragement" in the enclosed pouch — which was no longer enclosed — to an Englishman described only as Delphi who had provided useful intelligence to the United Provinces during the late war. Delphi was being instructed to make contact, the letter continued, but given the roundabout route such an instruction would take, it was possible that he would not receive it until after Wevers was in London. Wevers was to ask him some questions about the large ships now in building on the Medway, the supply of information having dried up over the last six months.

Arlington and I looked at each other.

'Well, Master Mercurius,' Arlington finally said, 'this explains a lot!'

There was a measure of suspicion attached to anyone Dutch, with the result that finding time to myself to gather my thoughts was not easy. However, I hit on the brilliant idea of going to the chapel, safe in the knowledge that the chances any Englishman would be going there must be quite slight.

I knelt in an attitude of prayer, but I confess that my thoughts were not particularly holy. In fact, they were decidedly infernal, because I was trying to think who Delphi might be. Whoever he was, it was likely that he had betrayed his country and would not want to risk that fact becoming known. He would have had good reason to kill Wevers.

On the other hand, if that was the motive, it had no connection to the planned marriage and therefore the rest of us would be safe. Wevers would be the only one who could identify Delphi, so he was the only one at risk.

Ah, I reasoned, but then Wevers did not know who Delphi was, so all Delphi had to do to stay safe was not to make contact with Wevers.

Ah, yes, I answered myself, but did Delphi know that Wevers did not know who he was, or might he have supposed that Wevers had been told that snippet of information? But then if Wevers had been told, Delphi might erroneously assume that others of our party knew it too.

I quickly glanced over my shoulder to check that I was still alone. I am not exactly a coward, but I look forward to dying in my bed at a ripe old age. Being found slumped in a chapel with a knife in my back did not appeal.

It was also preying on my mind that this had happened shortly after an attempt to disrupt the marriage negotiations by incriminating Preuveneers. Had the plotters decided that if one plot had failed, something more spectacular was called for? If not, must I ascribe the proximity of the two events to coincidence? The snag with that was that I do not believe in coincidence. And although I am not a Reformed minister — well, yes, I am, but in a half-hearted sort of way, given my Catholic ordination — it was not easy to shake off the idea that nothing happens by chance on God's earth. Predestination is a very handy explanation for all kinds of things if you want it to be.

You see, a coincidence is when two things happen in close proximity but you cannot see why they should be connected. This becomes more pronounced the rarer the events are. For example, if I say that every time I leave the university without my cloak it rains, that may simply reflect the fact that I often forget my cloak, and Leiden is a wet place; but if I say that I stopped walking along a path because a black cat suddenly stepped in front of me, and at that moment a barrel fell from an upper floor where I would have been standing, is that a coincidence? Unless black cats have ways of predicting what barrels do, I can't see how they can be connected.

However, if you believe that God intervenes in our lives, maybe coincidences are the way He does that. Perhaps He knows that I will stop if He sends a black cat to me. Since God is then the explanation for the apparent coincidence, there is no longer a coincidence.

Anyway, if the attempt to incriminate Preuveneers and the murder of Wevers were not coincidental, that meant there was a guiding hand behind them, and until I knew who it was I could not see that I was any further forward. I had to try to discover if anyone had attempted to spare the silversmith from his fate, but I was fairly certain nobody would have done.

I said a quick prayer, pushed myself to my feet and decided to return to my room to await Arlington's summons which, he had assured me, would be issued as soon as the King had finished breakfast. I had no idea what I was going to do until that happened, sometime in the early afternoon, though.

As it happened, someone had an idea about how to occupy me. I was sitting by the window in my room and had just opened a book when the door opened and Meg entered.

'Oh, I beg your pardon, sir!' she said when she saw me. 'I didn't expect you would be here.' She placed my laundered shirt on the bed. 'Is there somewhere else you'd like me to put that for you, sir?'

'No, thank you. I'll put it in my chest later.'

'Very good, sir.'

I had to confess I was impressed by her industry. I had only put that shirt out for washing that morning and already it was back, clean and well pressed.

Meg showed no sign of leaving. 'I'm sorry about your friend, sir. We just heard what happened.'

'Thank you. I didn't know him very well. We only met on the voyage to England.'

Meg nodded. 'Still, sir, if you need any consolation, please say.'

I may have mistaken her tone, but I was fairly sure that by "consolation" she had in mind something other than an arm round me and a shoulder to cry on. I must own that in the aftermath of what had happened, I wondered if this would be one of those traps you hear about, where a man is seduced into taking a woman into his bed and suddenly the door is flung open and her "brother" accuses you of various kinds of dishonourable conduct and threatens to tell all manner of people what you have been up to unless you pay a suitable compensation for the loss of his sister's virtue. You only needed a quick glance at Meg to realise that compensation for the loss of her remaining virtue couldn't cost you more than a farthing or two at the outside, but I would not want to run the risk of exposure. Van Langenburg might have turned a blind eye, William of Orange would probably have regarded it as none of his business, and the Rector would probably not have believed it. What really worried me was what my grandmother would say in such circumstances. It did not bear thinking about.

'Thank you, Meg,' I said, 'but I am bearing up thus far.'

She dipped in a curtsey and left the room. I returned to my book, but only after making a mental note to push my chest across the door when I retired at night. I was less worried about heavily-muscled ruffians than about a young woman whose dress displayed more meat than I had seen away from a butcher's stall.

CHAPTER NINE

It was around an hour later that there came a knock at the door and a page announced that Lord Arlington was waiting to conduct me to the King.

We met at the foot of the staircase and Arlington led the way.

'I regret that His Majesty's temper has not been improved by our discoveries,' Arlington murmured as we walked along.

Mistaking his meaning, I hastened to reassure him. 'I am sure that my countrymen will not lay the blame for this at His Majesty's door.'

'And I am sure that His Majesty does not care a fig about that, if you will forgive my plain speaking. It is the prospect of his plans being thwarted that concerns him. He has been speaking with his brother, the Duke of York, about the matter.'

Since the said Duke was having a loud and discourteous exchange with someone at the other end of the corridor, it was clear that the ill temper was not confined to the King.

I suppose that this is as good a time as any to record my impressions of James, Duke of York, the King's younger brother. These will, of course, be coloured by the recollection that he fought against my country, in particular at the Battle of Lowestoft where my brother was killed, and by the short space of time I was present in his company.

First, as to his laudable parts; I know of no man who doubted his personal courage. Quite apart from his military and naval careers, he had been very active during the Great Fire of London, as was his brother, organising bucket chains and supervising the destruction of buildings in the fire's path to try to break the onward movement of the flames.

Second, there was no doubt that he was utterly loyal and principled, at least in matters of religion. Despite his late father's dying wish, he converted to Catholicism out of a conviction that no other church could save a man's soul, and he resisted all threats and blandishments to return to the Church of England. He surrendered a number of offices of great profit rather than re-converting.

However, in this we also see one of his great weaknesses. James was utterly unable to determine between causes worth dying for and those of no lasting import, and could be remarkably stubborn for no sufficient reason. This might not have been a problem, except that Charles' courtiers could use the fact to their advantage. For example, Arlington and the Earl of Danby had won James' grudging consent to the marriage of his daughter to William by reminding him that it was the will of the King; having a high view of the Royal Prerogative, James could not oppose his brother even when it was to his disadvantage. While Arlington still believed that James might be behind the obstructions we were encountering, Danby did not, for precisely this reason; that once his brother had declared his will, James had no choice but to acquiesce. Having said that, Danby allegedly said that "the fun would start when James became King" because he would expect the same obedience.

I will add one other attribute that bears upon these events. James was not rated highly for his intelligence. At the Battle of Lowestoft, James was standing beside a man who was decapitated by a cannonball and was spattered with his brains; which, according to one writer, was the only time he was ever seen to have any brains about him. Charles had a certain cunning. I became convinced that this appearance of pleasure-seeking and devotion to women, feasting and the playhouse was true, but was exaggerated to serve the purpose of making others think that Charles was no threat. They discovered too late that he knew exactly how and when to strike. James, on the other hand, was the sort of man who might have held all the honours in a game of cards and still somehow managed to lose.

I have mentioned the Earl of Danby, who was strangely absent at this moment. Danby was the King's Lord High Treasurer and first minister, effectively the head of the government, and a staunch supporter of an alliance with our country. Danby's view was simple; he loved trade, upon which the prosperity of the Kingdom would be founded, and he knew that the French had nothing to offer in that regard. We, on the other hand, had the spice trade and missions in China and India, and upon the coasts of Africa. If our navies worked together, we could interdict any other nation. King Charles had taken some convincing, but once Danby had persuaded him, the invitation to talk about a marriage had soon issued. I did not know it at the time, but Danby was keeping away in order to force Arlington and others who had opposed the idea to have to take the lead in prosecuting the proposal. This way, they would have a reason for not wanting it to fail — and if it did, Danby would be able to say that his idea was sound but it had been botched by these saboteurs. You had to admire him; I had thought the De Witt brothers were shifty and self-serving, but next to Danby they were but amateurs.

Anyway, Danby had taken himself off to Yorkshire to attend to some urgent business on his estates. This, so Arlington claimed, was so that if the negotiations with us did not bear fruit, Danby could initiate some with France and protest long and loud that those with our country were nothing to do with him. There was also some certainty on the part of the French that, whatever rumours they may have heard, there could be no serious negotiations with us that would not involve Danby. In fact, Danby had cunningly arranged that the French knew nothing about our visit by inviting the French Ambassador to join a house party in Yorkshire which is, I understand, a distant part of the Kingdom cut off from all news of the court.

Unfortunately, there was no way of approaching Charles' presence chamber that avoided meeting the Duke of York, who was walking back and forth outside the room arguing loudly with one of his secretaries. When he saw us coming, he desisted, and greeted us with an extravagantly courtly bow, which the secretary quickly copied. Arlington was well able to reciprocate, but I have ever been ungainly and my posterior bears the mark of many a doorknob from my attempts to bow well, so I returned the greeting in the German fashion, clicking my heels together and ducking my head abruptly.

'Master Mercurius, I believe?' the Duke said.

'Indeed so, Your Royal Highness.'

'I understand that you have been introduced to my daughter by the Bishop of London.'

'I have, sir. She is a very accomplished young lady.'

'Isn't she?' James responded, with every evidence of satisfaction. This was a little surprising, because most noblemen of my acquaintance can barely tell you how many daughters they have and take little or no interest in them until the time comes to sell them into marriage, but the Duke appeared as proud as any common man might have been.

That appeared to have exhausted all useful intercourse between us, so James bowed once more and took himself off, resuming his discussion with the secretary further along the corridor.

I started to speak but was silenced abruptly by Arlington. After a few moments, he removed his hand from my mouth.

'I beg your pardon,' he said. 'I thought it might be useful to know what His Royal Highness was saying to that fellow Coleman.'

'His secretary?'

'Secretary to the Duchess of York. He is a fanatical Catholic, and all London knows he is in the pay of the French.'

'Ah,' I said, 'I see,' though in fact I did not.

'The Duke was insisting to Coleman that anyone who is involved in any plot to prevent the marriage is doing him a disservice. I really believe that he does not know who it might be.'

'But does Coleman?'

Arlington looked at me in a curious, appraising sort of way. 'You are not such an innocent as might appear, are you?' he chuckled. 'I rather think that the Duke wishes to use Coleman to get a message to whoever is behind this, and there would be no point in that if Coleman had no idea where to go looking, would there?'

I think it will be clear to any reader that I am not made for plotting. My head was spinning as we entered the King's chamber, and I was much tempted to announce that urgent business called me back to Leiden and leave it to someone else to sort this out, except that I could not think who that might be; and I was fairly sure that if I deserted my post, William would not leave me peacefully in my library but would send me back again with a less friendly scene on the quayside.

Charles was an imposing sight at any time, tall and in his prime, but he emphasised this when he wanted to by standing on a little platform that supported his chair. From this point he towered over us all, and I do not mind saying that the effect was very impressive. 'You are a dark horse, Mercurius!' he began.

I wanted to tell him I was not any kind of horse. I admit my nose is longer than some, but that is where the equine resemblance ends; but it seems he did not mean this literally.

'Van Langenburg has given me a letter from my nephew in which he tells me that you are an inquisitor of some ability.'

I proved the point by instantly asking myself why Van Langenburg had such a letter, unless someone in the Dutch party anticipated the events that had happened. On the other hand, and notwithstanding that pride is a terrible sin, it was good to know that the Stadhouder found my work satisfactory.

'Mercurius, I hope that you will do me the same service you have performed for William, and work with Arlington to find those responsible. If you succeed, you will not find me ungenerous.'

I could have sworn that Arlington snorted, but when I glanced at him he had a face like a statue.

'And, what is more to the point,' Charles continued, 'you will have earned my goodwill. We're always on the lookout for suitable bishops, aren't we, Arlington?'

I have already remarked that I was ordained as both a Reformed minister and as a Catholic priest. The idea that I could have a future as an Anglican bishop was just adding complexity to an already difficult life. Mind you, if I had foreseen at that moment what would happen when Charles died and James succeeded, given the knots James got into with his bishops, I might have signed up for a bishopric because there would be something delicious about being accused by a King of being insufficiently Catholic when you could prove you had been a Catholic priest for over twenty years. A lot of James' problems would have vanished if a friendly Pope had excommunicated him. They never do, of course; great men can do all kinds of things and the Pope just writes them a note excusing their behaviour. Consider the Duke of Orleans; most men who dressed in women's clothes and showed an unnatural interest in guardsmen would be on a gibbet in no time, but the Pope simply shrugged it off as high-spirited horseplay.

However, I digress (again).

Arlington was busily explaining the findings of the examination of Wevers' body to the King. My attention had wandered a little — I find listening to English requires a lot of concentration — but Arlington had produced a roll of cloth which he unwound to reveal the two daggers, in which the King showed the greatest interest.

'I think we might return his weapon to Mr Vlisser,' suggested Arlington.

'When he leaves,' the King countered. 'But tell me, was the other in Wevers' sleeve when he was received here on your arrival?'

'I believe it must have been,' Arlington answered.

Charles knitted his black brows in a considerable frown. 'Show it to the Captain of the Guard and ask him how his men missed it. It may step up their vigilance for a week or two.'

'It will be done, Your Majesty,' Arlington replied.

'Good. Now, Mercurius, what do you propose to do next?'

The question took me completely by surprise. I had been envisaging an inquiry in which Arlington took the lead and I threw in the odd helpful comment as things came to my notice. It was an unpleasant shock to discover that I was apparently in charge of the hunt for Wevers' killer.

'I think, Your Majesty,' I began, then ran out of anything to say.

'I'm glad you do,' Charles answered, 'but what do you think?'

'I think … that whoever is responsible for the accusation against Preuveneers may also be behind the death of Wevers, and therefore we should question the silversmith more carefully.'

'That will be difficult,' Arlington told me. 'He did not survive the last lot of questioning.'

This came as a surprise to me, but not to the King, or so it seemed.

'Well,' Charles sighed, 'if he would not tell us who had commissioned him to do the smaller thing, he wouldn't have given up the greater name either.'

'Indeed, Your Majesty,' said Arlington.

They spoke as if dying under questioning was evidence of a lack of moral fibre.

'Still, can't be helped now!' said Charles cheerfully.

'Then it seems to me that the best course of action is to demonstrate that the conspirators have once more failed in their objective and that the negotiations are proceeding well,' I suggested.

Charles looked doubtful. 'Are they?' he asked.

'They haven't really started,' Arlington answered. 'We've only held an introductory session to introduce each other.'

This was true. Unless matters were proceeding without my knowledge, we had spent most of our time in London eating and drinking.

'But the conspirators may not know that,' I said. 'Or, perhaps I should say, if we claim that they have gone well, we may discover whether the plotters are so well connected that they know otherwise.'

'Oh, very cunning!' said Charles, rubbing his hands together briskly. 'If they know no progress has been made, we'll know they're insiders, whereas if they're provoked into more action, we'll know they're not part of the talks. I like that.'

'Perhaps, sir, we might announce a provisional date for a celebration?' Arlington proposed.

'A party! Yes, that would do well. Not too soon, I think. Am I doing anything on Sunday week, Arlington?'

'Divine Service in the morning, Your Majesty, but we might amend that to a Service of Thanksgiving for a successful conclusion to our talks and then throw a banquet for our Dutch friends in the evening before they leave.'

'Excellent! Well, there you are, Mercurius. You'll have ten days to find the murderer before the party. If you succeed, we can end the whole thing with a hanging, and if you don't, you're leaving anyway so that will wrap the whole show up nicely.'

I was not sure that the idea of setting a limit on the inquiry was how these matters were supposed to be managed, but how could I argue with the King? William would have been immune to dispute too; he was very much his uncle's nephew. I just had to get on it.

'I will need to interview the Princess Mary again, Your Majesty,' I said.

'Why? Surely she isn't behind this?'

'No, sir, I meant as part of my duties with the mission.'

'Oh, yes. She's at Richmond, isn't she, Arlington?'

'Yes, sir.'

'Should we fetch her to town?'

'I think not, Your Majesty. The one sure way of preventing a Dutch wedding would be to abduct the bride. We must increase the guard at Richmond and restrict her movements.'

'Quite right,' said Charles, who now looked less happy. 'I hadn't thought of that possibility. My God, there are some evil people about. Arlington, ensure that Mercurius has a horse or carriage to take him to Richmond. And give him some money in case he needs to bribe a few people.'

This was definitely not the way that William would have proceeded; not that he was averse to bribing people to get what he wanted, but he did not often give anyone else any money to do it. In fact, I had heard his officers complain that they had to meet the cost of these payments themselves.

We bowed, and for once I managed to reverse out of the room without encountering any door furniture, largely because the guards on the doors ensured that they were drawn right back.

'So, Master Mercurius, what now?' Arlington enquired.

'To Richmond, I suppose,' I said.

CHAPTER TEN

The Princess was a very different young woman in her own surroundings at Richmond. Her younger sister, the Princess Anne, was there for company, though they squabbled as sisters often do, it being Anne's firm opinion that the household was run entirely for the benefit of Mary and that she, as the younger sibling, was held of no account.

Their governess was Frances Villiers, the wife of Sir Edward Villiers, whose own children were also to be found in the house, to the number of seven or eight. Most of them were older than Mary and could be accounted young adults, but Mary had some companions of her own age.

Mary greeted me very civilly. Her eyes were reddened, the result, as I learned, of copious tears due to the thought of being married at so young an age, though she was at pains to assure me that this was no reflection on the merits of my master. He was, after all, her cousin, and she knew him to be a serious and accomplished man, she told me. Certainly nobody could accuse him of being a fop or dandy.

'No doubt you will think me a silly girl,' Mary continued, 'for I know that it is not given to princesses to marry for love. But yet I am conscious of my tender age to have so great a decision made for me.'

'On the contrary,' I assured her, 'the fact that the importance of marriage presses upon you is proof that you are not a silly girl.'

Lady Villiers glided silently forward to offer a handkerchief to Mary to dry her eyes, and then returned to her chair in the corner. In the absence of the Bishop of London, I felt that a softer approach to the interview might be possible.

'My lady,' I said, 'my task is to enquire into your religion. The Prince of Orange cannot marry anyone who is not committed to the Protestant faith.'

In retrospect, this was a risky suggestion, because all she had to do was announce herself to be a Roman Catholic and the wedding plans would have died on the spot, but instead she rushed to reassure me.

'Master, you will not find any lack of zeal for the faith in my sister or myself. And Uncle Charles has been insistent that we must be loyal and obedient members of the Church of England.'

'You will forgive my remarking that your father is a Catholic, and there must be pressure to follow his example,' I answered.

'By no means, Master! Uncle has explained to us that the people distrust Catholicism and would remove our family from the throne if they felt that we were all Catholics. They may bear one Catholic so long as the succession is secured to Protestants thereafter, and therefore it is important that we girls remain firm in the faith.' Mary opened a small book on the table beside her. It was her own notebook in which she had recorded some prayers and devotional thoughts, which she offered to me to read. 'You may see, Master, if my beliefs are not entirely Reformed.'

I turned a few pages and read a little, leading me to two conclusions. First, that there was no cause for concern about her religion, and second, that she may have been the most abominable speller of her age.

On the voyage to England, Bouwman had been good enough to remind me of an episode in English history which bore upon our mission, and this seemed to be the right moment to broach it. The previous Queen Mary had married Philip of Spain and had insisted that he must be regarded as King, at least during her lifetime. This had been extremely unpopular with the English people, who, to this day, disregard him in any list of monarchs. It was necessary to discuss the position of my master if the marriage took place and Mary should subsequently ascend the throne. This would, no doubt, be discussed by Van Langenburg and King Charles, but I wanted to know Mary's view on the matter.

'Why, Master,' she exclaimed, 'I will be his dutiful wife. It is unthinkable that I should occupy a higher rank than my husband. 'Twould be against both God and nature.'

Bouwman's view was that this would satisfy William very well. He would never be King of the United Provinces because our country is a republic, but he could be a king *in* the United Provinces, with all the honours pertaining thereto. My concern was what happened if Mary predeceased him, as women so often do due to the travails of childbirth, and he was then expected to relinquish his title and crown. He would then return to the Netherlands and would be exposed to the bitter tongues of his enemies as an ex-king; and we must never forget that her father had a new wife who was of child-bearing age. It was not impossible that Mary of Modena would provide him with a male heir, thus demoting Mary in the order of succession.

I was turning all this over in my head when it was stamped upon by a simple consideration. *Mercurius*, I told myself, *this is not your world. You are a university lecturer. You do not understand all this. What are you doing even thinking about it?*

A few seconds served to dredge up the names of people of humble origins who had involved themselves in politics, and just a couple of moments more to recognise the key unifying factor between them. They were all dead, and some of them were not nicely dead, if I may put it that way.

I know we all have to die, but I hoped to do so at an advanced age, preferably in my own bed and ideally during my sleep. Too many of those other fellows had met their ends violently and in messy and painful ways. I thought of the De Witts, for example, and realised that I like having my innards on the inside, not draped across the cobbles of a square in The Hague. If I needed a closer example, I had only to think of poor Wevers, breathing his last in a squalid back lane in a city far from home.

It was at this point that I resolved to get home to Leiden as quickly as possible. My job was to decide whether Mary was a fit woman for William to marry, and the answer was an unequivocal yes, so all I had to do was write my report and get on the first ship across the North Sea. I didn't even mind if it was heading for Hamburg. I enjoy a good walk.

'Was there anything else, Master?' Mary asked.

I reddened to realise that I must have been sitting in silence while all these thoughts crowded through my head. More to the point, my face frequently betrays my cogitations, so it was quite possible that the young princess had been observing my expressions and worrying about whatever lurid and disturbing ideas I might be having. 'No, Your Royal Highness, I am entirely satisfied.'

She smiled for the first time. I am susceptible to a woman's smile. It warms me strangely. Of course, I have taken a vow of chastity, so the idea of a close attachment to a woman, however attractive, is quite out of the question.

Well, when I say "out of the question" I mean "not possible". Not if the bishop finds out about it. I will not deny that there have been women — a *small* number of women —

who have excited feelings in me that were, perhaps, more tender than I should have liked. And it was true that my grandmother, unaware of my ordination in the Catholic church, fretted on the subject of my lack of a wife. On the rare occasions that I was able to visit her, she would slyly insinuate it into the conversation, usually before I had managed to get my travelling cloak off. Subtle hints such as "Have you found a wife yet, Mercurius?" or "I suppose I am doomed never to be a great-grandma" followed by a deep sigh peppered our conversation.

[My clerk, Van der Meer, sniggered when I dictated that bit about "a small number of women". I shall remember that when I share out my worldly goods at my end. He'll be lucky to get my second best Bible.]

'May I ask something, Master?' asked Mary.

'Of course,' I replied.

'Tell me something of your country,' she said. 'If I am to live there, it would be as well to know something of it.'

It goes without saying that we Dutch know that our land is the pinnacle of God's creation. After all, God made a start on it, since which time we Dutch have made new bits by building dykes, digging canals and draining polders. Give us enough time and you will be able to walk from The Hague to England, though why anyone would want to defeats me.

'It is a very fair country, ma'am,' I said. 'It lacks mountains, but it has pleasant meadows and beautiful gardens, and its cities are delightful. There are many fine houses, and the Prince has no great love of city air and prefers to be in the countryside as much as possible.'

This was true, by the way; the Prince suffered from asthma and found the smoke of cities irritating to his lungs. He resided at The Hague as little as he could get away with. At one time he felt it was necessary to be there to watch out for plots, but he came to realise that it did not matter if he lived somewhere else so long as he let it be thought that he was in The Hague. Thus he would sometimes ride to one of his country houses after dark, having ensured that he had been widely seen in the city during the day, then he would quietly return the following day as if he had never been away.

'Will I be permitted a household such as this?' Mary asked.

'It is not for me to say,' I answered, 'but my master is a kindly man, and he would wish to see you well provided for. I believe your aunt had no ground for complaint when she married his father.'

The family tree of royal families is never straightforward, but it was true that when Mary married William her aunt would also become her mother-in-law. Except that she was dead; but you know what I mean.

'When I come to the Low Countries,' Mary continued, 'I shall need a Chaplain. Perhaps you would consent to serve me, Master.'

It sounded more like a command than a question, and one that I had not anticipated. I could see a number of reasons why that would be a very bad idea. First, a good Protestant princess should have a good Protestant chaplain, not one who was actually a closet Catholic. My bishop was very tolerant of the deceits necessary to maintain secrecy about my conversion, but I think becoming a royal chaplain would test that amiability to the full; though, in truth, his predecessor would have thought it a capital joke.

More importantly, I would have to live in The Hague, which was altogether too close to William for my liking. I would be drawn into all those things I had hoped never to have to trouble myself with again; exactly those matters I had been thinking about only a few minutes earlier. My life would no longer be my own.

I had to come up with an alternative quickly. 'Wouldn't you rather have an English chaplain?' I asked.

'The Bishop of London would not come,' she answered. 'He has too much to do here. And if my husband is not a member of the Church of England, surely it is my wifely duty to worship alongside him in his church?'

'Ah. Yes,' I stammered. 'Certainly. A wife should worship with her husband.'

Have you ever had that feeling that you were digging a hole and that all your attempts to stop were causing you to dig deeper?

Suddenly, inspiration struck.

'And in due time,' I continued, 'that is undoubtedly the best answer. But the services will be in Dutch, and it will take some little time for even as gifted a lady as yourself to master our language. In the meantime, you should have the consolations of religion provided by a man of your own nation.'

Mary considered this for a moment. I knew that she was thinking hard, because she chewed her lip. 'Yes,' she said eventually, 'I can see that. Perhaps I should ask the Bishop to recommend someone for the moment, and we can look at this again when I have learned Dutch.'

By which time, I thought, *I shall have returned to Leiden; or possibly entered a monastery. Either way, I shall be nowhere near The Hague.*

A door opened and a young girl ambled in. It took no introduction to realise that this must be the Princess Anne, given the resemblance to her older sister.

Lady Villiers tried to usher her away, but Anne resisted. Whatever was going on in our room was obviously much more interesting than anything else she could be doing.

'Who's this?' she demanded, pointing at me.

'Don't point!' barked her sister. 'And especially not at Master Mercurius.'

'Mercurius? That's a funny name.'

'It's a Dutch name,' Mary explained. 'He's Dutch.'

I did not feel it appropriate to point out that it was actually a Roman name. It was also the original name of Pope John II, who was the first Pope to adopt a new name upon his election. No, nobody seems to find that as interesting as I do.

'What's he doing here?' Anne asked.

'He has been sent by our cousin William to see if I am a suitable wife. If arrangements can be made, I will be married to William.'

'You? Married? You're not old enough.'

'I'm very nearly fifteen. Plenty of princesses are married long before my age. Aunt Mary was only nine when she married William's father.'

Anne considered this for a moment. 'Has William got any brothers?'

'Why?' asked Mary.

'Well, then I could marry one and go on living with you.'

Mary looked to me for the answer.

'No, I'm afraid not. His father died when he was born,' I said.

'That's a shame,' said Anne, then, feeling that conversation was exhausted, she announced, 'I'm going now,' and left us.

Conducting an assessment of the Princess before marriage was daunting enough, but coupled with an investigation into the murder of a Dutchman on English soil, it was quite exhausting. Having been given only ten days to complete my investigation, I felt I could not take any time to sit and read in my chamber. I had to be doing something at every moment, or I would feel like an idler.

'I wouldn't worry too much,' said Van Langenburg when I met him to report on my visit to Richmond. 'The ten days is unimportant.'

'But we are being told we will be leaving then.'

'And not a minute too soon in my eyes. But even if you have not laid the blame at anyone's door, Charles will simply find a scapegoat and hang him.'

'Isn't that unjust?' I protested.

'Oh, the fellow will be destined to hang anyway. Charles will tell him that if he confesses to the killing of Wevers his widow will get a few shillings, maybe even a pound, and his body won't be anatomised. That's quite an attractive offer for a man under sentence of death. Over here, the usual thing is to cut your head off and divide you into quarters for display on the city gates. That's if they don't disembowel you alive first.'

Now, I am not an expert in these matters, but I could see that avoiding a public disembowelling had its attractions, especially if your wife was going to get some silver into the bargain, but I was less clear about the quartering thing. 'If you're hanged and beheaded, I don't think you'd be too worried what happened next,' I suggested.

'Ah, but the common notion is that at the resurrection of the dead you will need a body, and if the body has been broken into parts, you cannot be resurrected,' Van Langenburg explained.

You would not expect me to have no view on this, and I do. It is piffle.

It is true that when Our Lord was raised He returned with a physical body and proved it by allowing people to touch him. It is also true that the Epistle to the Philippians says that Jesus will "transform the body of our humble state into conformity with the body of His glory" which strongly suggests a physical body. And in the nineteenth chapter of the book of Job we read "I know that my Redeemer lives, and at the last He will take His stand on the earth. Even after my skin is destroyed, yet from my flesh I shall see God." I could multiply quotations, but I think I have made my point. However, a God who can do this is not going to be hampered by the body being in pieces; and if one or two parts are missing, I am sure that He can supply some new ones.

However, I did not say this to Van Langenburg, confining myself to less theological observations. 'There is such a thing as truth,' I said, 'and I think we owe it to mijnheer Wevers to make every effort to identify his killer.'

'Oh, indeed! I would not suggest otherwise,' Van Langenburg hastened to assure me. 'I meant only that if God does not vouchsafe us an answer, we ought not to despair.'

I felt a little shamefaced at this. I had not thought to bring God into this enquiry because, quite frankly, His previous record when it came to helping me with my investigations was not what one might have hoped. I had done a deal of praying over previous cases without getting any obvious response; but it could not be denied that an omniscient Being would be a great assistant if I could just get Him to share His knowledge. 'I will redouble my prayers,' I announced.

'And I mine,' Van Langenburg added. 'Meanwhile, Bouwman is to return to The Hague to tell the Stadhouder all that has transpired. I have given him a report to carry, and King Charles has offered four soldiers to guard him on his journey. If there is anything you wish him to do for you, make haste, because he sails on the evening tide.'

I thanked Van Langenburg and retired to my chamber to write my report. The first draft was succinct but perhaps lacked courtly expression: "She'll do."

After a lot of thought and a flask of excellent French wine — how did they get that? — I was able to expand on this terse assessment to assure William that the Princess was comely, intelligent (in her own way), properly brought up and hygienic. This last was important because Dutchwomen have rather higher standards of cleanliness than most, and William would not want a wife who excited adverse comment at Court.

Now here is a strange thing — and I admit I digress again. Whenever I visit a Dutch home, it is very likely that the woman of the house will apologise for its shockingly untidy state as she admits me, even though everything is clean and the floor is well-swept. This admission of inadequacy will not prevent the same woman tutting over another woman's efforts, of course, and the greatest tutting is done by those lordly women who have never lifted a broom in their lives but have servants to do it all for them.

To return to the point, I was trying to think of a tactful way to tell William that his wife-to-be was now half a foot taller than him, so he might want to buy some high-heeled shoes for the wedding when I noticed Bouwman crossing the courtyard beneath me on his way to the carriage that was to take him (and his heavily-armed escort) to the ship. I quickly signed my letter and ran down the stairs with a view to giving him the missive, asking him to seal it himself when convenient.

As I sprinted across the courtyard towards him, I was perturbed when the escort suddenly jumped from the carriage and aimed their muskets at me. Fortunately, Bouwman had the presence of mind to yell that I was a friend, whereupon they reluctantly agreed not to shoot me. Having said that, I was over twenty paces away so they might well have missed anyway.

'Thank you,' I gasped as I regained my breath. 'My death would have been rather inconvenient at the moment. I have so much to do.'

'It would also have annoyed King Charles,' Bouwman commented, 'especially since it would have been his own men who did it.'

'I suppose it might be regarded as an unfortunate lapse in standards of hospitality,' I agreed. 'I have written a brief report for the Stadhouder. No doubt you will brief him about poor Wevers.'

'The less there is committed to paper, the better,' whispered Bouwman. 'I do not know whom to trust here.'

'You may trust me,' I said.

'I wasn't worried about you,' said Bouwman, and he clapped me on the arm and mounted the carriage. He was gone before I thought to ask him the obvious question.

If not me, then just who was he worried about?

CHAPTER ELEVEN

At intervals, I become acutely aware of my limitations. I never wanted to investigate crimes. I have had no training in it, and it has occasionally crossed my mind that it would be prudent to foul up the occasional case so that people would stop asking me. The difficulty with that approach is that I owe it to the victims to give my best efforts, and that nobody asks me anyway. Usually they tell me I have to do it.

I had noticed that even though I was not one of his subjects, King Charles was taking it for granted that he was entitled to order me about, and I had no doubt that if I had protested the Stadhouder would have told me to stop whining and get on with it. Although William would have denied it fiercely, he was very much his uncle's nephew and they were more alike than he was prepared to believe, and certainly more alike than anyone was prepared to tell him to his face. Both believed that their interests and those of their country exactly coincided, and therefore any patriotic man should exert himself to meet his ruler's demands because only a traitor would not; and since anyone with a brain knew what happened to traitors, Charles and William usually got their way. They certainly did with me. The fact that I believe in life after death doesn't mean that I want to be proved right anytime soon.

And, let it be said, the funny thing is that having lived to be over eighty, my desire to hang around a while yet is not one whit diminished.

Anyway, as Bouwman left I decided the best thing I could do was to find a chapel and do some praying. This is not decrying my own intellect. I found that as I marshalled my thoughts for prayer, quite often the mere act of doing so tidied up some loose ends and helped me to see what my next act should be. Of course, I would not have been much of a priest if I had not hoped that one of the saints would whisper something useful in my ear while I was on my knees, and I did a lot of petitioning to St Jude, the patron saint of desperate causes. He was certainly in the forefront of my mind as I climbed the stairs from the courtyard and asked one of the guards how to find the chapel. It turned out that he thought he knew, but he was wrong, and in no time I was at the front door of the palace.

I could see the imposing abbey in the distance, but that was too grand and busy for my purpose. However, I could see a smaller church close by that looked as if it might afford some peace and privacy, so I took myself off down the road and settled myself on a pew to think.

I did not fall asleep. Not for more than a few moments, anyway. But whether awake or asleep, something popped into my head. I said earlier that I do not believe in coincidence, so if somebody changes a routine on a day when an event happens, I ask myself whether there is a connection and, if so, what it could be; and the germ of an idea was forming in my brain.

To test it out, I needed to go for a walk, and I needed to do it at once. I said a quick prayer of self-commendation, asking God to keep me safe, then stepped outside. It was already late afternoon, and since I did not choose to perambulate London's streets in the dark, I had to step out quickly.

The first task was to remember the way to St Martin-in-the-Fields. This was less troublesome than is usually the case when I have to rely on my sense of direction. Standing beside it, I turned to face the river. I could see a street leading in that direction, but before following it I mentally marked the nearby inns and taverns. There were a couple to my right and another across the street a little to the left of the church. London was full of places to get drunk, so it was not impossible that there were others that I could not see, but I reasoned that Wevers would have seen what I saw, so if he had wanted to escape Morley this was where he would have gone to do so.

I walked down the street towards the river. It was bustling with carts making their way to a patch of land on the outskirts of town called the Haymarket. The city needed large amounts of hay for its horses, and the poor quality of the roads outside its gates meant that many farmers preferred to deliver their hay by barge, only using carts for the last part of the journey; and the nearest part of the river was in front of me, just outside the walls of the Whitehall Palace precincts. So far as I could see there were no gates on that side of the Palace grounds, the nearest one being at the top of Whitehall leading into Scotland Yard.

So here was a pretty puzzle. As I had expected, Wevers had stuck to a well-populated route on his way to the Savoy. He would never have entered the alley by choice, and it was unlikely that he had been stabbed there because the act of pushing him into the alley would have put him on his guard and given him precious seconds to draw his dagger. Even if he had not had time to use it, it was inconceivable that he would not have drawn it had he felt threatened.

And yet … there was probably no busier part of London, but nobody had reported seeing anything. I had to assume that the constables who gathered there on the night of the stabbing had done their job of questioning bystanders diligently, so either there was an enormous conspiracy or somehow the assassin had managed to sneak up on Wevers without arousing suspicion, and even more remarkably to do so from the front, and had then manoeuvred the body into the alleyway without anyone spotting them in the act, before finally making their escape covered in blood, again along one of the busiest streets of the city.

I had a strong impulse to get myself a large goblet of wine.

The King's penchant for keeping irregular hours meant that the kitchens in the Palace never slept and you could get something to eat at almost any hour, so although dinner had ended when I arrived in my chamber, the servants were just about to start serving supper. So far as I could tell, supper was almost indistinguishable from dinner. You just had to drink faster to keep up with the food.

I sat at the table. Vlisser was eating at the far end, but he was already surrounded by company, as the rich often are, and I did not feel the need for companionship while I was thinking. I was slowly chewing a hunk of bread when I became aware that someone had slipped into a place beside me.

Since the somebody in question was wearing a dress of dusky pink silk, it was either a woman or the Duke of Orleans, and as I was fairly certain no state visit was in progress that ruled him out.

We had not been introduced, but a quick glance told me that this was a member of the royal family. It was not so much a physical similarity, though that could be seen, but something about the way she looked at me that reminded me forcefully of Charles.

I made to rise to my feet, but she put her hand on my arm to press me back down.

'Nay, sir,' she said, 'I did not mean to disturb your meal. Pray continue.'

I offered to pour her some wine.

'Thank you, but I have had my fill. You looked lonely sitting there, and I thought it inhospitable to allow a visitor to our shores to dine alone.'

'You are very thoughtful, madame,' I said. 'I do not believe we have been introduced. I am Master Mercurius of the University of Leiden.'

'I know,' she said. 'I'm Charlotte.'

'Charlotte...?'

'Oh, you want a surname. That's a bit complicated. It keeps changing, you see. I started as Killigrew, or sometimes Boyle, then I became FitzRoy, then Howard, and now I'm Paston. My father-in-law is the Earl of Yarmouth. It's all terribly complicated. And just a little bit dull.' She giggled rather fetchingly. 'Oh, don't worry!' she said. 'I'm not going to seduce you. My husband wouldn't like it.'

I looked around the room. 'Which gentleman is he?'

'He isn't here. He's gone to look after his estates in Norfolk. I prefer to stay here. At least London isn't flat.'

'My country is very flat, madame. I am quite used to it.'

'Well, lucky you. I'm glad to say I'm not flat, don't you think?'

If this was the standard mode of conversation with clergymen in England, there was more need for reform than I had believed. I suddenly felt rather warm.

'Dear me, you're blushing. My father said you were very strait-laced.'

'Do I know your father?'

Her eyes opened in mock horror. 'Which part of "FitzRoy" didn't you understand?'

I am a dullard sometimes, and the cogs of my mind turned very slowly for a moment or two. 'Oh!' I said.

'Oh indeed. I'm one of the King's Acknowledged Bastards.' She pronounced the name as if it were some kind of exclusive club.

'One of them? Is it a big society?'

Charlotte mulled over my question for a while. 'I think there are fourteen of us, but who knows what the old goat has been up to lately? He is remarkably energetic.'

I was shocked. It is telling that my first thought was to wonder if William knew about this, because I was very sure he would disapprove. 'You are remarkably open, madame,' I said.

'Not really. Everyone knows. I didn't see why you should be left out.' She reached forward and adjusted my collar, which must have become disarranged. Her fingers lingered on it as she smoothed out a crease. 'My father wants you to enjoy your time in England.'

'Oh, I am,' I rushed to assure her, probably unconvincingly. *One of us has been murdered and I've got less than ten days to find out why and by whom*, I thought, but decided not to say it for fear of being thought an ungracious guest.

'Well, if there's anything you want…' Charlotte whispered breathily.

'I'll be sure to tell the maid,' I completed her sentence.

Charlotte wagged her finger. 'Naughty boy!' she said. 'You'll get the pox.' She looked round the room. 'Which one is she, anyway?'

Meg was filling pitchers of ale in the buttery, but I pointed her out as she set them on the tables.

'She must be new,' said Charlotte. 'I don't know her.' She smiled at me sweetly. 'You're probably all right, then. If she's new, she won't be as poxed as the others.'

Charlotte stood and glided away, pausing only to trail the ends of her fingers over my shoulders and give me a little tinkly wave and a smile. I was probably staring at her a little too long, because I did not notice anyone approaching until another hand landed on my shoulder.

'You're in there,' announced Vlisser.

'How do you mean, mijnheer?'

'She's yours, young man, anytime you like.'

'She's a married woman,' I observed.

'So was her mother when the King laid with her. It doesn't count for much here.'

'It does with me,' I replied with some heat.

If the truth be told, I was rather cross with myself. I was a Catholic priest. I had taken a vow of celibacy. I could hardly tell everyone that marriage is an honourable estate and then lie with a married woman. All this weighed against any intimacy with Mrs Paston.

And yet that smile, and the distinct "non-flatness" of her, had almost unnerved me. My resolution had been wavering. No wonder I was mad with myself.

'The women here are very forward,' Vlisser observed.

'They certainly are,' I agreed. 'Do you know, on the very first day my maid offered me ... well, never mind what she offered me. Let us just say they were personal services.'

'Oh?' said Vlisser. 'Which one was she?' He craned his neck to look round the room.

'The one in the brown dress.'

'Most of them have brown dresses.'

'With a white apron.'

'They all have white aprons. Some cleaner than others, admittedly, but they all started white.'

I had never really looked at a maid before. They are just anonymous figures in an interior. Of course, they are individual human beings, but while they are working they do not register with us.

I was reminded of my mother wiping her hands on her apron. There were always two or three clean ones in the press ready for use. She used to say that it didn't take much to wash an apron, whereas a woollen dress was very difficult to clean. Meg wore an old-fashioned collar about her shoulders, almost large enough to be called a shawl, and tied with laces at the front. Compared with the ladies of the court, she was a picture of modesty.

'How have your enquiries progressed, Master?' Vlisser asked me.

'I begin to see a little light,' I told him truthfully. I had no idea whether it was a distant bright light, or a feeble light close by that would soon be snuffed out, but it was better than total darkness.

Charles sent for me in what he called "the late evening" and the rest of us termed "the middle of the night". I hurriedly donned my clothes again and followed the servant to the King's private suite.

'I'm sorry, sir,' he said, and pulled my arms upwards, stroking my sleeves for concealed weapons. 'Orders,' he explained.

Charles was lying on his bed, wearing his nightshirt and slippers. A young lady was asleep beside him, wearing neither of these things.

Charles followed my gaze and smiled. 'Ah, you haven't met the Duchess of Portsmouth, have you? It's probably best if I introduce you formally another time, don't you think?'

'If Your Majesty pleases.'

'I thought we might have a little chat,' the King explained, easing himself off the bed and heading for a flask of wine on a side table.

I may have appeared rather confused, because my grasp of English was not secure and I thought he had said "a little cat".

Charles pushed a goblet in my hand and indicated a chair where I might sit. 'No ceremony, Mercurius, no ceremony! This is man to man stuff. I'm not your monarch.'

'No, Your Majesty.'

'How have your labours succeeded today?'

I noted that the possibility that I had not succeeded at all had been resolutely excluded as an option. 'I believe I see a possibility, but I need to speak to the man Morley.'

Charles swirled his wine round his goblet. 'Is that absolutely necessary?' he asked.

'I believe so.'

Charles turned this over in his mind for a few seconds, then strode to the door, opened it, and commanded one of the guards to send for Lord Arlington. There was quite a delay, presumably while His Lordship dressed, but eventually he appeared in the doorway looking more than a little dishevelled and missing the patch on his nose.

'Arlington, I want you to arrange for Mercurius to interview Morley.'

Arlington appeared shocked. 'Forgive me, Your Majesty, but is that wise?'

'Why wouldn't it be?'

'Well, the man is a spy. His work will be compromised if his appearance is known.'

'Then sit him behind a screen or something of the sort. God's wounds, must I think of everything myself?' Charles exploded. 'I wonder sometimes why I bother with ministers.'

The lady on the bed stirred at the sudden noise and opened her eyes. If I had expected her to shriek with horror at the discovery of two strange men in the room, I was sadly wrong. The Duchess simply turned over, had a leisurely scratch and went back to sleep.

Arlington accepted the inevitable. 'Very good, Your Majesty.'

'Excellent. Well, off you trot. Some of us have things to do.'

He did not specify what those things were. He didn't have to.

CHAPTER TWELVE

Morning came, and I experienced once more the daily disappointment of realising that this was not all a horrible dream.

All I wanted was a quiet life. I yearned to sit once more in the university library or, even better, take a book from the library and enjoy it in Jan Steen's inn on the Langebrug. I was even beginning to feel nostalgic for Albrecht's cooking. Admittedly that feeling only lasted a few seconds before I came to my senses.

It was not just we Dutch who wanted to be home. Our English hosts had cut back on the hospitality, allegedly out of respect for Wevers but more likely because the banquets were expensive. The prospect of going home in a little over a week was comforting for everyone. Except me.

I could not think how I could conclude a successful investigation given the handicaps of being a foreigner in a strange city. I had an idea — two, actually — which might turn out to be correct, but I was unsure how I could ever prove my suspicions to be right. It was then that I had a stroke of luck; or, if you prefer, Providence lent me a hand.

Van Langenburg, Preuveneers and I were walking in the gardens when we were greeted by a man walking towards us, and in our language too.

He introduced himself as Samuel Biscop, Minister of the Dutch Church in London. You may imagine how astonished I was to hear that there even was a Dutch church in this God-forsaken city, let alone that it had apparently been there over a hundred years. At one time there had been thousands of Dutch people in London, but the benevolent rule of William had lately encouraged many to return home. Even so, the congregation was very substantial, and when Biscop had heard of our arrival, he had looked for an opportunity to welcome some of his countrymen.

I cannot tell you what a pleasure it was to converse in Dutch once more after trying to get my tongue around the barbaric English language. Biscop was equally pleased to meet another Protestant minister — no, I didn't tell him my little secret — and over a pleasant half hour we compared our impressions of the English.

I made the mistake of asking Biscop what he thought of the state of English morals. In retrospect that was a stupid thing to say to a Calvinist minister, especially one whose constant concern it was to maintain the separate Dutch nature of his flock, and mijnheer Biscop discoursed at some length on the matter, apparently without the need to breathe between sentences. However, I cannot deny that his revelations were enlightening, because I now knew who was reputed to be sleeping with whom, and if I had possessed a large enough sheet of paper I might have been able to set down the many relationships in some kind of spider's web of sin. The King alone had a bevy of mistresses that the most depraved Sultan in the East would have envied for his harem.

Van Langenburg excused himself to keep an appointment with the King, although I doubt that was true because it was not even eleven o'clock, and Preuveneers did not choose to walk outside the walls of the Palace gardens given what had happened to him before, so Biscop and I strolled alone down Whitehall and I took the opportunity to glean some local knowledge from him.

I explained the awful fate that had befallen Wevers, causing me to reflect that it was surprising that Wevers should meet his contact in a busy place like the Savoy rather than in the sober surroundings of the Dutch Church.

'Perhaps he did not know of our presence here,' Biscop suggested.

'He said he had not been to London before, yet he seems to have known of the Savoy,' I responded.

'He could see the Savoy from the river. Our church is in Austin Friars, in the east of the city and not easily found,' explained Biscop. 'More to the point, it is above two miles from here. He could hardly go there and back without being missed, since he would be gone above an hour and a half.'

'I wonder whom he was meeting? Presumably an Englishman, since I cannot imagine the English would employ a foreigner and allow him access to any of their secrets.'

'True, but there are many who consider themselves Dutch but grew up here, as I did myself. We can pass as English if we want to. One would suppose that whoever arranged the rendezvous between mijnheer Wevers and the other gentleman believed that they would have a common language. Did Wevers speak English?'

I thought hard. 'I don't think he did,' I said at length. 'He had to ask Bouwman to translate when he spoke to the sergeant who was attempting to arrest Preuveneers.'

'Well, then,' said Biscop, 'that must narrow the field. Although there are many Englishmen who learned Dutch during the King's exile.'

Now we begin to get somewhere, I thought. It was obvious once it was pointed out to me. Who would the King trust after so long away, if not the people who had stood by him during his exile? And the spy who was so much use to us would have to have been trusted by the English, or he could not have passed on much of value.

Biscop kindly invited me to his church on the coming Sunday, and I engaged myself to be there if at all possible, and so we parted, he to return to his duties and I to go down on my knees before Almighty God and thank Him for sending such a civilising influence amongst the English.

A servant brought me a message from Lord Arlington suggesting that I have an early meal so that I could meet Morley at two o'clock, when I would be sent for. I cannot say that I was particularly hungry; in fact, I rarely am. That is one of the blessings of working in a place that employs Albrecht as master of the kitchen. However, I made my way to the dining-hall and had part of a game pie and an apple washed down with some beer.

At the appointed time another servant appeared, and I was led through the various corridors and walkways and through a formal garden to another mystifying collection of rooms that turned out to include Lord Arlington's office — and, next door, the King's private laboratory.

Arlington was waiting for me in the laboratory. 'You will, I am sure, understand that certain steps have to be taken,' he said.

Not knowing what he meant I said nothing, which served to make him appear even more nervous.

'I must ask you to wait here for a minute after I leave you,' he explained. 'Mr Morley is in the adjoining room behind a screen. If you will put your questions to him, I will convey his answer.'

'He will not speak for himself, then?'

'It is better this way. We must take every measure we can to maintain his secret identity. I'm sure you understand.'

I certainly understood that Arlington was being as difficult as he might, though I had no idea why. But two can play at that game.

I nodded my acquiescence, and Arlington thanked me before passing through the door. His servant stood resolutely in front of it just in case I was not a man of my word.

In due time the servant stood aside and let me pass through to Arlington's office. A large black lacquered screen in the Chinese style was placed in front of the window with Arlington standing at one end and a bulky servant, with his back turned to Morley, at the other. There was a chair in front of the screen where I was invited to sit. In view of the setup, I was tempted to begin by asking "How long is it since your last Confession, my son?"

One of the other lecturers at Leiden has a favourite technique for testing the candidates at viva examinations. He likes to begin by asking the most difficult or unwelcome question first. I have never liked the practice, because a candidate who struggles at that point will not show at their best, but it seemed appropriate here.

'How have you enjoyed your days in the dungeon, Mr Morley?'

It was clear that Morley had no idea what I was talking about. Despite Charles' order to Arlington to lock him away, it had not been done. I knew that, of course; anyone who has spent two days in a dungeon will not lose the stench of it in a day.

'If you cannot answer that question, Mr Morley, I have others. Please tell me what happened when you followed mijnheer Wevers on the night he died. How did you know where to find him?'

There was some whispering behind the screen, following which Arlington spoke.

'Mr Morley says that he was informed that the party was going to walk to St Martin-in-the-Fields and there to go their two separate ways, so he waited there in the shadows. Having been furnished with a description of Mr Wevers, he knew whom to follow.'

If it were true, then it was unlikely that Morley had anything to do with the incident with the silversmith, but I was not convinced that he was telling the truth.

'And then, Mr Morley, you somehow lost your mark within only a minute or two of beginning to track him. How did that happen?'

I could hear a disapproving snort as if Morley's professionalism was in question, but he whispered again to Arlington.

'Mr Morley tells me that Wevers crossed the street to a nearby inn where he stepped inside. After a few moments Morley followed, but could not see Wevers therein. He walked around the inn but realised that Wevers was not there.'

'This was the inn to the left or right as you look out from the church?'

'To the left, I am informed.'

'And there were no other exits?'

'There was one at the rear, Mr Morley says, but barrels had been stacked behind it so that nobody could sneak in unobserved. Nobody could have left that way.'

'I see.'

Actually I did not. It was true that the back door might have been barricaded, though when I poked my head around the door there was no obstruction. What took some believing was that Morley had not seen at once that Wevers was not there. The inn was very small.

'So,' I continued, 'what did you do when you realised you had failed in your mission?' I was being deliberately provocative to see if he would come out to throttle me and reveal himself.

'Mr Morley says that he retraced his steps and ran to the corner. He could not see Wevers in any direction. After a few moments of indecision, he walked down the road towards the river.'

'Walked, not ran?'

'He did not wish to draw attention to himself.'

That rang true, but Arlington gave the answer without waiting for Morley to speak.

'And did he see Wevers' body in the alleyway?'

There was some whispering again.

'He did not look,' Arlington told me.

Now I was very suspicious. What spy would walk past a dark alley and not look, if only for his own safety?

'Were there any closed carriages in sight?'

More low speech followed, and this time Arlington obviously asked a question of his own in order to elucidate the facts more clearly.

'Mr Morley says that there were several hay-carts and at least two carriages, one coming up the road and one heading down. It is, he thinks, possible that Wevers had entered the carriage going downhill, which would explain why he could not be seen.'

'And in which direction did the carriage go when it reached the river bank?'

'Mr Morley says that it turned to the left, towards the Savoy.'

'Did he follow?'

There was an animated discussion during which I could almost hear Morley's words myself.

'Mr Morley says that he attempted to do so, but the carriage was too swift. By the time he reached the bottom of the hill it was near a furlong ahead, and he did not choose to make a spectacle of himself in public by running.'

It was, I suppose, possible that things had fallen out as Morley said. Wevers might have entered a carriage, willingly or unwillingly, but if the latter, why was his dagger not drawn? Unless, I suppose, it was a woman's carriage, when his suspicions might not have been aroused. Then he might have been done to death elsewhere and his body returned. But then we had the same problem as with Vlisser's weapon; why not leave the body in the carriage, or dump it in the river after dark, instead of bringing it back to the road where he had been abducted?

And why would he enter a carriage anyway when he had an appointment to keep? I had not known Wevers long, but he seemed to me to be single-minded of purpose. If he had a task in hand, he was not the sort of man to be deflected from it. I could not think of any inducement that would entice him to climb into a carriage in a foreign city.

Unless, of course, the appointment was in the carriage. Wevers would certainly not have suggested such a rendezvous, but perhaps he was not in a position to make such a stipulation. Maybe the place and time of the meeting was to be determined by Delphi, though how that was to be transmitted to Wevers was unclear.

Think, Mercurius, think!

It was impossible to think during an interview, but I felt that Morley was not going to give me any more useful information.

Indeed, his whole purpose in this discussion appeared to be not to give me any useful information of any kind.

I had one potential trick up my sleeve, for which I was indebted to a colleague, Master Hubertus. Hubertus taught mathematics, and could best be described as a little eccentric, or, if you lacked Christian charity, barking mad. During interviews he was wont to throw in a question that had no apparent connection to anything that had gone before. At first we thought this was a clever trick to try to throw the student off his prepared path, but I came to realise it was probably because Hubertus' mind just worked that way. Asking a student who was busy developing an argument from Euclid's geometry whether he preferred strawberries or raspberries certainly served to show who was able to return to the subject after such a disruption to their train of thought, but I think Hubertus' motive in asking was at best unclear, except that he had a chart in his room which tabulated the numbers preferring each soft fruit. The last time I saw it, strawberries had a substantial lead in the contest.

'Mr Morley,' I asked, 'have you ever been to my country?'

This was a question of the simplest kind that afforded two possible answers, yes or no, and I did not expect it to pose too difficult a test, but Morley did not answer at once. I decided I must have disconcerted him more than I intended, but he whispered furiously to Arlington, who responded in kind.

'Mr Morley says that he does not see the relevance of that question to your enquiries,' Arlington said.

Except that I was sure that Morley had not said that. His whispering was loud enough for me to pick out a key phrase. He had asked Arlington what the answer was.

I thanked them both for their courtesy, at which Arlington asked me to leave first, undertaking to seek me out in a few minutes. The servant stepped forward to conduct me away, but I knew where I was going and I had no intention of waiting for him, so I rushed forward and opened the door to the laboratory myself. By pushing it behind me as I left, I slowed the servant so that I could run ahead. Achieving the door to the garden, I quickly slipped out onto the path and looked in at the window of Arlington's office. As I expected, Arlington and Morley were arguing about something.

Now that is interesting, I thought, as I recognised a familiar face. Why had Arlington recruited Captain Hallow to masquerade as Morley?

CHAPTER THIRTEEN

I had believed that Arlington was dealing honestly with me, but now I had clear evidence that he was not. I had thought that he had not imprisoned Morley, but perhaps he had, and that was why he needed to have Hallow impersonate him; or, I thought with dread, maybe Morley was another of the witnesses who would mysteriously die before I had the opportunity to interrogate them.

There were so many unanswered questions pressing upon me.

First, who was Delphi, and how had he managed to communicate with Wevers without the rest of us knowing?

Second, if we were right about Wevers being bound for the Savoy, where had he been killed? I had assumed he had been killed in the alleyway, but if so why had he not defended himself?

Third, who detailed Morley to follow Wevers? More importantly, to whom did Morley report? And whom could I ask, if Arlington was not to be trusted? Could it even be Arlington himself?

Fourth, the suggestion that Wevers shrugged off his follower by hiding behind a door in an inn that was not on his route, and no bigger than a large closet, was frankly laughable. So why did Morley lie about it? Even if Hallow had repeated the story, Arlington had given it to the King earlier and had presumably had it from Morley himself.

Fifth, it seemed a remarkable coincidence that within an hour or so of Morley being set to follow Wevers, Wevers had been murdered, and I have already explained my feelings about coincidences. Did Morley have a hand in the killing and merely claim to have lost touch with Wevers to deflect suspicion?

Sixth, we had been assuming that the motive here was to cause tension between our countries, thus putting the successful completion of the marriage negotiations under threat; but what if this was simply one spy dealing with another spy?

And yet, I thought, surely spies abound. Whatever he was going to do, at the time of his death Wevers had done nothing. If all the spies in London were to be used in this way, the streets would soon be choked with dead foreigners. Did someone know that Wevers was on his way to meet Delphi? But if they did, then surely the English would have wanted to know who Delphi was, the better to prevent his wicked schemes, so why not wait until after the meeting to kill Wevers, or even kill both Wevers and Delphi? Preventing a meeting at which the identity of an English traitor would be revealed made no sense at all, even in my naïve view of the world.

Seventh, what did they put in that game pie, because my bowels were in confusion?

Thus required to pass some lengthy time in the privy closet, I was not in my room when Arlington came looking. I did not know this, of course, except that when I emerged and went to my room to wash my hands I could see signs of agitation in the courtyard below the window. I quickly dried my hands and ran to one of the windows in the corridor which could be opened, and there I could hear Arlington ordering his men about.

'I want you to find that damned Dutchman!' he yelled. 'Bring him to me!'

When he used the adjective, I do not believe that he intended any theological reflection on the future of my immortal soul. I think he was just annoyed with me for some reason.

It seemed to me that if my absence was in some way unsettling to the English, then I had better remain unfound for as long as possible and therefore resolved to look for some hiding place where I could remain undetected for the greatest time. One candidate immediately occurred to me. I could go to the library. It was full of books, so no well-bred Englishman would spend any time in there.

Unfortunately, the point that I had overlooked was the King's great interests. While Charles had several large wardrobes to hold his clothes, he did not appear to have a library, and I did not want to draw attention to myself by asking a servant where it was. I tiptoed around the Palace for a while, peeking into corridors to assure myself that they were empty before venturing along them, but I must have toured much of the main building without finding anything that looked remotely like a library.

It was then that I heard a rustle behind me and looked in vain for some niche in which I might conceal myself.

'Why, Master Mercurius!' said Charlotte. 'Whatever are you doing?'

'I was looking for the library, madame,' I said, bowing awkwardly. I never bow any other way, to tell the truth.

Charlotte took me by the hand. 'This way!' she announced briskly, and we walked along the corridor, up a small staircase and along another corridor until we came to a door which Charlotte opened.

'There you are!' she said, and I stepped inside.

I heard the click of a key turning in a lock.

'Madame, there is some mistake. This is not a library.'

'No, it's my bedroom,' Charlotte said. 'But you never know, you may yet find it educational here.'

I hope that readers who have perused my journals to this point will have decided for themselves that this was information of the most perturbing nature. I will not deny that at this point I felt more than a little uncomfortable.

My family were not wealthy by any means, but when I was young the minister of my village, a man of excellent discernment and abundant charity, determined that I would benefit from an education and arranged for me to attend a school. I applied myself and he then — somehow — persuaded some leading men to endow a scholarship so that I could go to university. It sufficed to provide my fees and my maintenance, but there was nothing left over for carousing (and a good thing too, if you ask me). You may therefore understand that by the time I graduated I was, shall we say, inexperienced in the jousts of Venus.

Then I became a lecturer and, at the age of twenty-six, a priest, and from that potted biography you can understand why the forwardness of Charlotte Paston was causing me to erupt in a cold sweat. I thought for a moment that I should swoon, but that smacked too much of the innocent bride. I was, after all, nearly forty years old at this time; blushing insensibility was unfitting to my sense of decorum.

Charlotte came very close to me. The only thing that prevented her coming any closer was her substantial bosom.

'Sir,' she whispered, 'you can do me a great service.'

Now, I am not very familiar with idiomatic English, and I am afraid that I may have misconstrued her meaning. I thought that she was hinting at something of the animal breeder's yard.

'Pray, sir, promise me that you will make no noise.'

I was not prepared to engage myself thus far until I knew what she proposed to do with me, but she seemed to take my agreement for granted.

'Let us sit upon the bed here.'

No maiden ever sat with her knees more tightly clamped together than I did then.

'My father tells me that you are skilled in elucidating the truth.'

I did not want to answer until I knew where this discussion was going, but since the silence was extended and it appeared that no progress would be made without my assent to this proposition, I replied. It came out rather more huskily than I intended, perhaps because I was a little tense. 'His Majesty is very kind.'

'My husband is up to something.'

'I am not sure that I have any skills in detecting adultery, madame...'

'Adultery! Who said anything about adultery?' she snapped. 'William doesn't have it in him to commit adultery. I am more than capable of meeting all his carnal needs.'

I felt that some comment was expected. 'I do not doubt it, madame.'

'He is a young man, Master Mercurius. But his main interest is in the gaming table. That is his passion and his true love. I suppose if a woman were prepared to play at brag naked he might be momentarily interested in her, but otherwise I have no worries on that score.'

'I am pleased to hear it, madame.'

'No, my concern is that he is mixed up in something political. I am worried for him because he does not have the head for it, and I fear that he will finish up in prison — or worse.'

'Why do you suspect this?'

'Master, I will be frank. My father is only forty-six years old, but the life that he leads is sapping his strength. The Queen is not able to give him an heir. Clearly this is not the King's fault — the evidence for his virility is sitting beside you now — but men's thoughts are turning to the succession. There are two camps. One believes that the King's younger brother, my uncle James, Duke of York, must ascend to the throne. That is the time-honoured principle, and since the King's very Restoration was a vindication of that principle the King himself is insistent that his brother should succeed.'

'But others have reservations?'

'To some, Uncle James' papist leanings render him unfit to rule this country. They are looking elsewhere. Some favour his daughter Mary, but she is very young and would need a Regent. Others look to your master William as the leading male of the family. And of course if the planned marriage goes ahead, those two parties might be able to unite. However, a third group favours the Duke of Monmouth, my half-brother. As the son of the King they see him as fit to rule, though he is a bastard.'

'And you think your husband is involving himself in this? On whose side?'

'Oh, William has rarely expressed an opinion of his own in his life. But lately he has observed once or twice that the tide is turning in Uncle James' favour, and that a man who nailed his colours to that mast might do very well in the coming years.' She seized me by the arm. 'I know what you are doing here. And I think our interests coincide. My husband has expressed the view that the future peace of the country requires that Mary should not marry your master.'

This was news indeed! Here, for the first time, was a plausible candidate as the murderer. 'And where is your husband now, madame?'

'I told you, in Norfolk. Or so he says.'

'You think that may be an untruth?'

'It may, Master, it very well may.'

'Then the first thing to do is to establish whether he is actually there. You must write to him, madame, something that requires an immediate reply.'

'What kind of thing might I write?'

I thought for a moment. Who knows what a young wife writes to her husband? I blush to think.

'I know!' she said. 'I'll tell him I think I am with child again.'

'Will he reply to that?'

'He will if I tell him I need fifty guineas for new dresses.'

'And when he discovers that you are not with child?'

'Oh, that'll be months yet. I'll cross that bridge when we get to it.'

I was relieved that I was not going to be imposed upon to remedy the deficiency.

Charlotte unlocked her door and peeped out. 'All clear!' she said. 'I'll let you know when he replies.'

I agreed and stepped out into the corridor.

I had taken all of five steps when I came face to face with a guard.

'Ah, there you are, sir,' he said. 'My Lord Arlington is looking for you.'

It is true that I was not outside Mrs Paston's bedroom door, but if I were challenged I had no idea what else there was in the corridor where I could have been.

The guard was smirking, but I endeavoured to ignore him.

'Taking a chance there, sir!' he chuckled.

'I beg your pardon?'

'I mean, I'm sure you being with the lady was entirely respectable but still — with her husband not a quarter of a mile away…'

'Mr Paston is here?' I realised as soon as I said it that my excitement might be misunderstood. 'I mean only that I had understood that he was in Norfolk,' I added.

'Just got back, sir.'

'His wife consulted me on a spiritual matter,' I rushed to explain.

'Yes, sir. And you weren't there long enough for anything else. Completely understand.'

'How do you know how long I was there? Were you watching me?'

The guard appeared offended. 'Me, sir? Good heavens, no! Lord Arlington wouldn't be so jumpy if anyone was watching you.'

I felt relieved to hear that.

'No, sir, Mr Paston pays me to watch his wife.'

Arlington was decidedly agitated. I could see him pacing back and forth in the courtyard as he waited for me. I wondered why that might be. Was he concerned that despite his best efforts I had actually discovered something?

'Master Mercurius!' he cried, upon the instant assuming a sunnier disposition. 'I feared we had lost you.'

'I am sorry to cause you any concern,' I lied. 'A necessary diversion, I'm afraid.'

I mimed washing my hands. It took Arlington a moment of two to divine my meaning, then he smiled.

'Ah!' He came closer to whisper. 'There is an office of ease in the corner that the gardeners use. Much better than letting them foul wherever they wish.' He wrapped an arm around my shoulder and began walking me towards the main part of the palace. 'His Majesty is about to announce the success of his negotiations. It may be useful if we observe the reactions of the audience to see who shows disappointment at these tidings.'

It was a good plan. 'Excellent,' I said. 'You can watch from the front and I can look from the side.'

'Better than that,' Arlington answered. 'I'll be at His Majesty's shoulder, and I have arranged for you to be in the gallery above.'

'I didn't know there was a gallery,' I replied. 'I hadn't noticed it.'

'Well, perhaps gallery is too grand a term for it,' Arlington conceded.

He was right. There was a small passageway designed so that workmen could get to the mountings for the chandeliers, and a spyhole had been crafted at some time so that, if I laid on my stomach in the crawlspace, I could see the hall below.

Arlington followed the King into the hall and glanced up at me while His Majesty took his seat. The courtiers had clearly been told that the King was going to say something important, because they fell quiet at once. At least four women busily fluttered their fans before holding them open over their hearts, which I understand to be a sign of the engagement of their affections. The King seemed to spot them all. Mrs Paston was the last to rise from her curtsey, thus ensuring that she was noticed. Next to her stood a young man with a deep frown. It turned out that he often had this knot in his brow, because William Paston seldom understood what was going on around him. He was not a stupid man, but he was not inclined to take the trouble to do any research on anything beyond the gaming table and the bloodstock lines. I watched him particularly to see whose eye he tried to catch. It seemed likely that if the King's speech perturbed him, he would look to a fellow plotter for a hint as to how to respond, and I did not mean to miss that.

The King cleared his throat, and then decided to stand. This was a good move on his part; already taller than many men, when he stood on the dais he towered over his hearers. It was more than a little intimidating. When he did so, I could see that Van Langenburg was standing at the left side of the throne, mirroring Arlington's position on the right. Clearly they meant to present a united front to those present.

'We are delighted to announce,' the King said, 'that the negotiations with our Dutch friends have come to a successful conclusion. A few minor points remain to be fixed, but we will now proceed to issue an invitation to our well-beloved nephew, William, Stadhouder of the Republic of the Seven United Netherlands, to come to London at his earliest convenience to marry our niece, Her Royal Highness the Princess Mary.'

There was a polite ripple of applause, in which the Duke of York joined, albeit a few seconds after everyone else. I noticed that Mary was not present to hear her future determined.

Paston was clapping like everyone else, but his head was turned to the side. I followed his gaze, and thought at first that he was looking at the Duke of York, but then Charles invited his brother to come forward to receive congratulations as the father of the bride, and I realised that the object of Paston's mute enquiry was that man Coleman.

Coleman was not amused. He applauded when everyone else did so, but unenthusiastically, and I could see his lower jaw sliding sideways as he was in the grip of some fierce emotion.

Having said that, the Duke of York did not look one whit happier, but came to the King, who invited him onto the dais. Charles announced that James would say a few words.

To his credit, James did not say that his brother was a scheming manipulator who cared nothing for the feelings of a young girl and her injured father. Instead, he took a moment or two to marshal his thoughts before speaking, then addressed the room with a clear, confident voice. 'The world knows that I desire nothing more than the peace of this Kingdom,' he began, 'and the work done here today will ensure an end to wars with the Dutch Republic while sending notice to the world that we have a formidable ally. If the marriage of my daughter to my nephew achieves this, we must all rejoice, and I do so.'

There was more applause, though Coleman and Paston were just as unenthusiastic as they had been before.

The King ushered Van Langenburg forward. The small problem that Bouwman, his usual translator, had gone back to The Hague meant that he looked around for an alternative. Arlington carefully avoided catching his eye and Van Langenburg could hardly ask Arlington's Dutch wife, which would have been entirely improper. As a result, Van Langenburg said a few words in French, after which everyone applauded again.

The King then told us that there would be a celebratory banquet the following evening before we went home.

Just a moment — before we went home? I thought I had another week or so to complete my enquiries, but now I was being told that we were all going home imminently.

I rushed from my uncomfortable spyhole to see if I could have a word with Arlington, and if I could I knew exactly which word it was going to be, unusual though it was for a priest to use it.

He was speaking with the King so I held back, but the King spotted me there and called me forward.

'Well, Master Mercurius,' he said, 'you must be pleased with the success of the negotiations.'

'I am, Your Majesty,' I said. 'Anything that tends to peace between our countries can only be good. I was just a little perturbed to hear that we would be leaving so soon.'

Charles waved his hand dismissively. 'Oh, don't worry about that! It'll take a few days yet to get the formal letter of invitation written, pack your things and get your ship ready to sail with a suitable friendly escort of our ships. Besides, putting out to sea in the morning right after a banquet is never a good idea. If it looks like it's going along too quickly, I'll just find something in the letter I don't like and get it rewritten.'

Arlington patted me on the shoulder. 'It's standard diplomatic practice. Announce the conclusion then work backwards to get the agreement,' he said.

'So you haven't actually agreed the wedding?' I mumbled.

'Oh, yes, that was never in doubt,' Charles said. 'There's no reasonable alternative. Everybody knows that.'

'We were worried that you might be contemplating a French marriage,' I blurted out. I probably ought not to have said that in case it undermined our negotiating position, but I am no diplomat. For a start, I can't lie to save my own neck, and that seems to be an essential skill for such men.

'To whom?' asked Charles. 'The only unmarried male near the throne is the Duke of Orleans' son, and he is only two years old. Can you see me marrying Mary to someone who can't reach to her garter? He might do for Anne when the time comes, I suppose. But given the known habits of the Duke of Orleans, I am not convinced that Philippe is his son anyway. Did you know the Duke hopes one day to be Queen?'

Arlington and the King laughed uproariously. Of course, everyone in Europe knew it. I was tempted to ask whether Charles would be giving back the millions of écus he had received from King Louis over the years, but it did not seem politic, so I just smiled weakly at their jest.

I said earlier that I do not believe in coincidence, but I do believe in the hand of Providence, and it reached out at this moment. Lady Arlington tripped over, and Lord Arlington could hardly ignore her since she was only ten paces away, so he went to help. This left me alone with the King, and that allowed me to ask a question that I could not trust Arlington to answer.

'Your Majesty,' I asked, 'who gives Mr Morley his orders?'

'Morley? Why, Mr Coventry, I suppose.'

I had not heard the name before, which must have showed on my face, because the King raised an arm to the horizontal and pointed to a man who was issuing instructions to some clerks near the door before wandering off to talk to someone more interesting than me. Just then Arlington returned, and I could hardly run over to Coventry in front of him.

'Can I help?' he asked suspiciously.

'Thank you,' I said, 'I was just asking who Mr Coventry was, of whom we have heard so many good things.'

That was, perhaps, not entirely true. In fact, I had never heard of him.

'He succeeded me as a Secretary of State when I became Lord Chamberlain,' Arlington explained. 'A sound man.'

I subsequently discovered that there were two Secretaries of State. One looked after the south of the country, and the other was banished to the north. Coventry had been the northern one, and was now the southern one.

'I am pleased to hear you say so, My Lord,' I said, 'for I understand he is Morley's superior.'

Arlington turned a funny colour, as if he had swallowed a grape and discovered it to be a sheep dropping. 'He is,' he conceded. 'All intelligence matters come within his purview.'

'Then, by your leave, let us ask him what he knows of Morley's activities,' I replied, and crossed the room without waiting for a reply.

Arlington introduced me to Mr Coventry and explained that I was investigating the death of mijnheer Wevers at the King's command.

'Ah, yes,' Coventry said. 'I heard about that.'

I suppose he would not have been much of a head of intelligence if he had not, since it happened not a quarter of a mile from where we were standing and it had been the talk of the court ever since.

'I understand, Mr Coventry, that Wevers was being shadowed by a man named Morley, who unfortunately lost sight of him shortly before his death.'

It was abundantly clear from Coventry's face that this was the first that he had heard of it. 'I assure you, sir, that we are not in the habit of following the citizens of friendly nations.'

'Am I to take it, then, that this was a jaunt of Mr Morley's own?'

Coventry was not such a fool as to answer directly. 'It was not authorised by me,' he said. 'I will make enquiries upon the matter.'

'It may help you to know that the King was aware of it,' I said guilelessly, then I bowed politely and left Arlington and Coventry to have what I believe diplomats like them call "a robust discussion".

CHAPTER FOURTEEN

Vlisser had a mind to take the air outside the palace one last time before we left, so I said I would accompany him. To my surprise, he went first to a passage alongside the great hall where a large map of London was hanging on the wall.

'I did not know that this was here,' I admitted.

'I wouldn't go out without looking at it,' Vlisser announced. 'You'd never find your way round this city without one.'

It was easy to find the palace and St Martin-in-the-Fields, and I could see the route Wevers must have been following to the Savoy. But then something leaped out at me.

'Mijnheer Vlisser! Would you indulge me? I want to check if this map is entirely accurate.'

Vlisser made no demur and soon we were walking along Whitehall. When we reached St Martin-in-the-Fields, we turned towards the river and finally entered the alley where poor Wevers was found. We walked along its noisome length, wading in filth, but I assured Vlisser it was in a good cause.

I found a crate and stood on it so I could see over the fence to my left. It did not tell me what I wanted to know, so I suggested that we retrace our steps and return to the street, perhaps taking some refreshment in an inn I knew.

We sat in the tiny inn, Vlisser taking in the view of the street as he glugged his beer, and I watching the innkeeper at work at the far end. Eventually my patience was rewarded. The innkeeper sent his boy to get a fresh barrel and the back door was opened. Leaning slightly to my left, I could see out of the door into the yard behind. There was an outhouse of some kind, and a yard littered with empty bottles and kegs, and at the end there was a gate through which they must have received their deliveries.

'Will you have another?' Vlisser asked.

'I've had enough, thank you,' I said. 'We should be getting back for dinner.'

'Should we?'

'And the drink will be free there.'

Vlisser was not a rich man for no reason. In no time he had grabbed his hat and cloak and we were striding back to the palace. 'Did you learn anything?' he asked.

'Oh, certainly,' I replied. 'English beer is horrible. And expensive.'

'That's true,' Vlisser agreed. 'Still, our trip has not been entirely fruitless. We have arranged a marriage, and I have found myself a supplier of excellent English wool.'

'How did you do that?' I asked. 'We have barely set foot outside the palace.'

Vlisser tapped the side of his nose. 'It's all to do with whispers. That's how business is done, Mercurius. You let it be known that you're in the market for something, and that there's a healthy commission for someone who brings it to you. Then you sit back. I've seen three major merchants since we've been here.'

'But you don't speak English,' I said.

'No, but I speak money, and that's a universal tongue. If there's a deal to be made, I'll learn a little Russian if I have to. And the Englishmen are the same. Everywhere in the world, Mercurius, a man who holds up some silver gets people's attention. They fall over themselves to be his friend.'

'I thought you were negotiating Mary's dowry?'

'That was straightforward. The English have got next to nothing to give us, but I extracted a few concessions and trading rights. Dutch ships will be able to trade at any English port without punitive excise duties, and vice versa. And to be honest, all William really wants is to stop Mary marrying a Frenchman. Any dowry he gets is a bonus. Charles loses anyway; he has been receiving a hundred thousand a year from Louis XIV, and you can't imagine that will continue after Mary marries William.'

'I suppose not. But I hate to see the blessed sacrament of marriage reduced to a business transaction. Whatever happened to marrying for love?'

Vlisser looked me up and down. 'I can tell you're not married,' he said. 'What's love got to do with it?'

Solitude. That's what I was missing. I do my best thinking on my own. Other people's views sometimes help, but not very often. Usually I can work things out for myself, given some time and space to think; and that was just what I was not getting in London.

It was partly my fault. By the time I got to my room at night I was too tired to do much thinking, and when I got up in the morning I wanted to start investigating at once. I could have stayed in my room until midday like the King and most of his courtiers, but I absolutely refused to change my habits to accommodate such laziness, or, rather, the late night revelry that caused it.

I admit that I am not an early bird. I have never quite understood why someone decided that we should start the day with prayer at six o'clock in the morning rather than nine o'clock, which would be a much more sensible time; but I put on airs compared with most in Charles' court.

Anyway, on this particular afternoon I decided I needed to find somewhere to be alone, and my room was the obvious place. I climbed the stairs and pushed the door open to find Meg with a handful of my papers.

'Beg pardon, sir,' she said. 'Just tidying. Would you like me to do it later?'

'Yes, please,' I said. 'I have some work to do.'

She bobbed a curtsey and replaced the papers, but could not resist giving them one last squaring up before she bobbed again and left, giving me a shy little smile as she squeezed past.

I do not know whether having a suspicious nature is ungodly. It is certainly uncharitable; but I was interested to know what she had been looking at. The uppermost papers on the desk were my cogitations on the fourth of Pascal's *Lettres provincials*, in which Pascal castigates those who believe that a person does not sin if they do not know their actions to be immoral. Fascinating though my ideas were, I could not think that they would attract the attention of an English maid, particularly since they were, of course, in Latin. I do my best thinking in Latin.

If not those, then perhaps she had replaced them on the pile to conceal the item beneath that she was reading. I riffled through the papers to the last of my notes, then lifted the stack to reveal some scribbles I had been writing on the matter of Wevers' death, but they were fragmentary, incoherent, and in Dutch. What use would those be to a young girl who had shown no sign of understanding our language?

I was assuredly worrying unnecessarily. After all, most young Englishwomen of the lower classes could not read. Maybe she really was just tidying, as she claimed. Or perhaps her interest was not in my papers, but in my valuables. My chest was still locked, and I had my pouch about me, so my cash was safe.

No matter. I decided to begin with a period of prayer and dropped to my knees. I opened my Psalter and read Psalm 72, where my eyes fell upon verses 18 and 19: *Verumtamen propter dolos posuisti eis; dejecisti eos dum allevarentur. Quomodo facti sunt in desolationem? subito defecerunt: perierunt propter iniquitatem suam.* Which means: truly you set them in slippery places; you make them fall to ruin. How they are destroyed in a moment, swept away utterly by terrors!

If only it were true that the wicked of the world did not prosper! I know that this is corrected in the life to come, but it would be good if God occasionally smote someone for being miserly. Having conceived the wish, I decided not to stand too close to Vlisser in case God answered my prayer with a thunderbolt and his aim was off.

But my mind returned to that word *terrors*. What was Wevers' killer frightened of? Men do not kill others for no reason, and this was no vulgar robbery or tavern brawl. This was a planned murder in the street. Whoever killed him could not have had any interaction in the time available other than to draw his dagger, and that so swiftly that Wevers did not see it. And if this was a planned killing, then someone knew Wevers would be there or followed him and somehow got ahead of him. It seemed incontrovertible that the murderer knew where he was going, at least in general direction.

My first idea was that the murder was simply an escalation by those who did not want the wedding to succeed. Having failed to get Preuveneers jailed, they took the life of Wevers, and that was the theory that we had proceeded with.

But when you thought about it, this made little sense. Not to put too fine a point on it, killing any of us would have worked as well. If I were an assassin — and I am definitely not cut out to be one — I would not tackle a fit young man with military training. I would stick my dagger into Vlisser or Preuveneers, or even me, since I could be guaranteed not to be carrying a weapon. The fact that Wevers was picked out implied that this was not just a second attempt to disrupt the talks.

So was this just a coincidence of the type that I have decried earlier?

I scratched my head and thought hard. Let's say that person A tries to have Preuveneers arrested and fails. Now they need to do something more, but that will take some time to arrange. In the interim, person B stabs Wevers. Wouldn't A decide that he doesn't need to do any more for the moment, and wait to see what happens?

Of course, the death of Wevers did not stop the discussions which had now been successfully concluded, so maybe A would now be spurred into action again. Alternatively, they may decide that they had failed.

Now, approaching the matter from the other end: we know that Wevers was going to meet Delphi. It was an appointment that Delphi must have suggested because Wevers did not know who Delphi was, so Delphi would have known where Wevers was going. Was Delphi the murderer, then?

But why? Delphi had been supplying information to my government for some time, and must have been well rewarded for doing so. By killing Wevers, he would lose the opportunity for a lucrative new commission. Perhaps he had decided that he did not choose to spy for us any longer, but then all he had to do was avoid making any appointment. Taxed about the matter later, he could have lied and said the instruction to meet Wevers did not arrive in time.

Ah, but now we have another conundrum. How does Delphi communicate his discoveries to The Hague? There must be someone else in England who knows Delphi's identity, so why not get Wevers to meet him so that the offer can be passed to Delphi? We have to call the intermediary something, so let us name him Apollo, who was the god honoured in the temple at Delphi.

Why ask Apollo to contact Delphi to ask him to speak to Wevers instead of simply telling Apollo what we wanted? The obvious reason is that we do not want Apollo to know what Delphi is being asked; and why might that be?

I poured a cup of wine and stared into its deep red interior; and then it came to me.

Whoever Apollo was, he would not want Delphi to share the information being sought. Now, what was it?

Large ships being built in the Medway! That was it. The supply of information had been interrupted for a few months. Did someone in The Hague suspect that the material being collected by Delphi was being intercepted by Apollo? Of course, I had overlooked the matter of the missing pouch. We could be sure that Wevers had not kept the appointment, so Delphi did not have the pouch.

So now we had two suspects. Whoever Apollo was, he may have had some connection with the navy such that he would come under suspicion if the information leaked out, even though he had not personally supplied it. He would not want Wevers to get that information, or even to meet Delphi if that meant that Apollo's own role in blocking the spying came to light.

But why would Delphi himself intend any harm to Wevers? It wasn't as if Wevers knew who Delphi was.

That little spark lit up for me again.

Delphi might not know that. He might assume that Wevers had been told who he would be meeting; and if he had decided to stop supplying intelligence, maybe he feared that Wevers would come looking for him and expose him. Avoiding the rendezvous would not work if Wevers knew whom to seek out.

Well done, Mercurius! You had one suspect, and now you've made another one. Stop now, before you make matters worse.

CHAPTER FIFTEEN

The banquet was being set up in the Banqueting House, and I could see harassed servants running back and forth across the yard bearing platters or pushing carts with the heavier items on them.

One might have thought that staging a banquet at next to no notice would present a challenge for Charles, but his kitchens were worked hard anyway and I suppose if you feed a lot of people every day, feeding them more formally is not quite as difficult as it would have been for William, who probably did not even have the number of dishes and platters that would be needed.

William was not a gourmet, but neither was he a gourmand. He ate when he needed to, and as much as he needed to, and he disliked formal dinners at which he would be compelled to make polite conversation or, as he described it, waste time. The Princess Mary was not often to be seen at her uncle's banquets, I understood, otherwise she might have found the Dutch court an austere place. I have heard many epithets applied to my master over the years, but I never heard a man call him frivolous.

As it happened, the Princess had been summoned from Richmond to join the festivities so that her complete delight in the plans made for her could be demonstrated. I was unsure that this was wise, having witnessed her red-rimmed eyes a few days earlier, but perhaps she had been schooled in the interim and brought to understand the great honour that my master was doing to her.

William was not one for grand palaces. He would rather have three small ones than one large one, so Mary could expect variety of residence rather than excessive opulence. On the other hand, looking at the ramshackle condition of some parts of Whitehall, perhaps she would be pleasantly surprised by the Binnenhof. Around forty years before, plans had been drawn up by Mr Inigo Jones to completely rebuild Whitehall, but the purse of King Charles I had been inadequate to complete the work, and the Banqueting House in which we were now assembled was a sample of what might have been.

Since this was a special occasion, I had donned a clean collar and hose and shaved especially carefully. My hair was freshly brushed, though I declined the perfumed powder one of the servants offered me. As I entered the hall, I could detect that I was probably the only man who had done so.

With the ending of the Puritan ascendancy in England, the fashion for black and white had been supplanted by a more colourful approach, not restricted only to the ladies. Paston was wearing a suit of gold satin with an outrageous red feather in his hat, while his wife was more primly tricked out in dark blue and silver. Coventry, Compton and I were the only ones keeping to our black outfits; even Van Langenburg had adopted a scarlet sash and gloves, while Vlisser wore a gold collar of such dimensions that I was surprised that he could walk under it. I have seen prisoners in lighter fetters.

Having been commanded to be in place by five o'clock, I was surprised when the appointed hour brought no sign of the King, and said so to Van Langenburg.

'Oh, he's probably having a nap,' Van Langenburg answered. 'It gives him something to do between breakfast and dinner.'

Just then the Bishop of London appeared at my elbow. 'A word, if you please, Master,' he said urgently, and plucked me away with a nod of apology to Van Langenburg. 'I should be grateful for your help,' he said. 'There has been a most disturbing development.'

'Indeed? How can I assist?'

'The Princess Mary is most distressed. Someone has sent her an anonymous letter concerning the private life of your master. She is minded to show it to her uncle as evidence that your master is not free to marry.'

I gulped. To be honest, I gulped several times. 'But that is nonsense!' I exclaimed. 'He told me himself…' But did he? He only said he planned to marry. He did not say that he was not already betrothed. Would I have known about it if he were? Maybe not, but Van Langenburg would surely know. 'I must consult Van Langenburg,' I began.

'There is no time,' Compton urged. 'In any case, the Princess asked particularly that you should come to her. She will accept your word that this is not true.'

'Then I must see the letter,' I answered. I did not add "just in case it is true." Not aloud, at least.

Compton conducted me to a suite of rooms at the end of a gallery where the Queen's Wardrobe was housed and where the Princess had been dressing with the assistance of some of the Queen's maids. I entered, not without some trepidation at insinuating myself into a place of so feminine a nature.

It was not a picture of tranquillity. Her Majesty the Queen was there, displaying evidence of the highest anxiety and occasionally erupting in a string of Portuguese. I must allow that she was a comelier woman than I had been led to believe, and considerably thinner than was the fashion amongst English ladies, many of whom were stoutly built.

In one corner the Princess sat sobbing into a handkerchief that would have made an adequate sail for a small boat. I had not expected that the Princess Anne would be there, but she was, exhibiting her sisterly affection by gently patting Mary on the back.

'There, there!' she said. 'Pray do not take on so. I told you he was a monster. I shall not marry. Not a man, anyway.'

'You can't marry anyone else,' Mary explained through her tears.

'When you're Queen, you can do what you want,' Anne replied. 'I shall.'

I advanced and bowed with a gentle cough to betray my presence.

'Oh, Master!' Mary cried. 'I am so glad that you are come.' She reached for a paper beside her and held it out to me, convulsing once more in sobs and waving it wordlessly for me to take.

I have heard scholars remark that something is written in an educated hand. I do not know what they mean by that, because surely the fact that it is in comprehensible language rather than a child's scrawl means it is an educated hand; but here I could see that this was written by one who was used to writing. It was fluid, without blots or misspellings (so far as I could judge, since it was in English) and admirably to the point.

Let Your Royal Highness be advised that Prince William is not free to contract a marriage, having committed himself to a lady in his own land, by name Elisabeth van der Nisse. His party will deny this, of course, but it is so.

I was momentarily nonplussed, but then it dawned on me that the writer had confused two people. The mother Elisabeth was married and at least a decade older than William. Her daughter Elisabeth was far too young to attract his notice.

Whoever had written this had clearly never met either of them; he had plucked a name from an almanac or perhaps heard it mentioned in passing. It was, of course, entirely possible that during Charles' exile he had met the mother. I could not say for sure, though I will say that all I had heard suggested that Dutch women resisted his attentions much more vigorously than their English sisters.

All this was by the by; for now, my concern was to set the Princess's mind at rest.

'Your Royal Highness, this is all fiction,' I said with all the conviction I could muster. 'The Prince is not engaged, neither is the lady at liberty to be so, being already married.'

'But why would someone make up something like this?' the young lady asked.

There are times when providing comfort requires an elastic rendering of the truth, and this seemed to me to be one of them. 'Jealousy, ma'am,' I pronounced. 'I suspect that the writer is envious of your good fortune in securing such a noble husband.'

To my surprise, and gratitude, the Bishop of London backed me up. 'Envy of your fortunate state is entirely understandable,' he said. 'It is the lot of very few women to find so upright a man to marry.'

Mary dried her tears and forced a smile. 'You will forgive me, gentlemen,' she said. 'I am very young, and such wickedness is not something I have experienced before.'

The Queen appeared mightily relieved and offered me her hand to kiss, which I did. She said something to me in English, but I find English spoken by English people hard enough to follow; English spoken by a foreigner is beyond me, so I cannot tell what she said.

'I must powder my face again,' Mary announced, and began to redo her toilette in a very matter-of-fact way. In that moment, I could see that she and William would do well together. Neither had patience with fripperies and show, and both had a strong sense of duty.

Compton grabbed my arm. 'Come, sir, let us withdraw,' he murmured. 'This is not a place for clergymen to be found.'

We bowed and left, and I hoped nobody had noticed that I had kept hold of the letter.

I do not know whether it was an example of the English sense of humour, but the table plan for the banquet left me sitting next to Lady Villiers, except that Princess Anne insisted on swapping places so that she could sit between us.

Finding conversation with a young girl quite difficult to maintain, I resorted to offering her sweetmeats every time she began to speak, which stemmed the flow of noise but earned me disapproving looks from her governess.

'Come now, young lady, let that tartlet be your last,' Lady Villiers said sternly.

'I hate waste,' Anne announced, grabbing another from the platter before I had the chance to return it to the table.

'They won't be wasted. The grown-ups will eat them when they have finished with their meat, if there be any left.'

I had an idea I wanted to test. 'By your leave, Lady Villiers, may I ask a question of you?'

'Indeed, sir, please do.'

'I wondered if you recognised a sample of handwriting.'

I did not show the whole message, which would have seemed inappropriate given the setting, but folded it in half and half again so only a portion was visible. Lady Villiers examined it closely.

'I fear not, sir,' she said.

I was in the process of returning the letter to my sleeve when Princess Anne spoke. 'Of course you do, silly,' she said. 'That's Mr Coleman's writing.'

And, do you know, that was the name I had thought to hear.

Before I did anything with the information, I just needed to clarify one thing. If Princess Anne recognised the handwriting, why did Mary not do so? And if Anne did, why had she not said so earlier?

The answer was simple in the event. Neither had actually looked closely at the letter. It had been opened and read by one of their ladies, and when Mary had been given the letter, she was so emotional that she did not look carefully at it but merely confirmed that it said what her lady said it did.

I waited until I could see Arlington on his own and then advanced on him with a purpose.

'How are you enjoying the banquet, Master?' he asked.

'Very much, My Lord,' I replied, 'but I have something to discuss with you.'

'Now?'

'If possible. Let us find a quiet corner.'

Arlington looked at me closely and could see I was not to be deflected in my aim. 'Come with me,' he said, and led me to the garden from which I had seen Hallow at the window.

I produced the letter and handed it to him. 'The Princess Mary was upset to receive this earlier today. I need hardly say that there is no truth in the allegation.'

Arlington nodded. 'I knew Elisabeth van der Nisse when we were in your country. The notion that she would behave improperly is laughable.'

'Thank you for your confirmation,' I said. 'I am informed that the handwriting is that of Mr Coleman.'

Arlington's eyes flashed with anger. 'Is it, by God?' Then, having realised that this was not the sort of thing one says to a clergyman, he continued, 'I beg your pardon. Shouldn't have said that. But Coleman is a thorn in my side. He is a fanatical Catholic and devoted to the cause of France, but he has been protected by the Duke of York.'

'I observed them in an argument a few days ago.'

'The Duke was ordered by His Majesty to discharge Coleman from his service, which he did, but Coleman was then employed by the Duke's wife as her secretary. He continues to lobby for a French alliance, but this will see him ruined.'

'What shall we do with it?'

'We will take it to the King, but not now. Let us enjoy the evening, and in the morning we will share what we know.' Arlington led the way back to the banquet, pausing at the doorway to bend towards my ear with a smile. 'I may even find it in my heart to be civil to Mr Coleman tonight, knowing what awaits him on the morrow.'

I conceived it to be my duty to inform Van Langenburg in confidence of the letter so that it would not come as a surprise if he heard anything about it. He congratulated me on my clever deduction and walked away before I could point out that actually it was Princess Anne who had recognised the hand.

Arlington's secretary sidled up to me at breakfast and informed me that his master would be grateful if I could attend upon him in his office in a quarter of an hour. In order to ensure that I could find it without walking halfway round London, I persuaded him to sit and have a cup of tea with me. He accepted readily, tea being an expensive commodity in

England, and in due time we proceeded through the corridors and staircases together. I was delighted to see that I could actually have found my way myself, though this pride came before a fall when we were leaving to go to the King and I attempted to exit through a closet.

The King was actually two-thirds dressed when we arrived, lacking only his coat and shoes, but surprisingly alert considering the convivial evening he had enjoyed. We could hear gentle female snoring from the chamber behind him, which may have accounted for his good humour, though this rapidly dissipated when he saw the letter.

'Van der Nisse? Nonsense. I didn't get anywhere with her, and I'm perfectly certain my nephew wouldn't even have tried.'

There seemed to be nothing to say to this, but Arlington mumbled, 'Quite, Your Majesty.'

'Who wrote it, Arlington?'

'We believe it to be the hand of Mr Coleman, sir.'

Charles was generally an even-tempered man, but his equanimity left him. 'That fellow Coleman again! I will have him gone, Arlington. My brother will not defy me on this again. Send him to me!'

'Coleman, Your Majesty?'

'No, my brother, you fool! He can have the interview with Coleman. I cannot trust myself to do it.'

Arlington left to invite the Duke of York to join us. I dithered, unsure whether to leave or go.

'You! Stay!' His Majesty commanded.

I did as I was bid. Technically I was not his subject, but he had armed guards outside and a broad view of his prerogative powers. It is hard to conduct an argument about your rights successfully when your head is on the end of a pike.

'Are we sure that is Coleman's hand?'

'I cannot speak to it, Your Majesty, but your niece Princess Anne recognised it.'

Charles seemed to be calming down somewhat. 'Well, she is a clever girl. And she would have seen his writing many times, I suppose. How is your other enquiry going?'

'I make progress, sir. Once Mr Coventry informs me who was giving Mr Morley his instructions, we should be much wiser.'

Charles held his foot in the air so his valet could slip a shoe on. 'If Coventry prevaricates, let me know. He's a good man, but he wouldn't admit today was Friday until it was forced out of him.'

I didn't think it was Friday, but maybe it was in England. After all, they didn't use the Gregorian calendar like us. We were ten days ahead of them.

The door opened and the Duke of York walked in, regarding me with some suspicion. I bowed and carefully avoided any eye contact. This probably made me look shifty, but it eliminated some awkwardness.

'Your daughter Mary was sent this yesterday,' Charles barked. 'It's a clear provocation.'

It was clear from the look on James' face that he recognised the handwriting. 'You must believe that I had no knowledge of this,' he began.

'Oh, I do,' Charles told him, 'for if it were otherwise you would be the basest, most disloyal rogue of a brother a man ever had.'

'I will discharge him at once,' James announced.

'Do so,' Charles ordered. 'And no payment nor any sinecure. If he argues, let him know that his choice is to go quietly or to face a public trial.'

'On what charge?' James asked.

'He has had access to naval secrets, has he not? I'm sure we'll find one that has leaked out somewhere.'

'If I may withdraw?' James asked, and was waved away.

I raised a hand to attract attention like a little schoolboy.

'Yes, Master?' said Charles.

'Your Majesty, before Mr Coleman leaves it would be good to ascertain whether he was behind the silversmith's false allegation.'

'Indeed it would! James, tell him to report to Arlington before he leaves. Arlington, there's a man at the Tower of London who is skilled at extracting the truth with a bit of mechanical help, if necessary.'

They all have them. I had seen one at work, and I never wanted to see it again. Having seen Coleman, I expected we would have a confession about half an hour after the torture master started work, if not earlier.

CHAPTER SIXTEEN

How quickly things can change. When he woke up that morning, Edward Coleman had a well-paid job as a secretary to the Duchess of York with access to some of the greatest men in England. By midday he had lost that job and all hope of another like it, and by mid-afternoon he was sitting in his undershirt strapped to a chair while one of the Constable's men heated a poker and a branding iron in a brazier. You will understand that I did not see this for myself, but it was explained graphically by the Constable when he made his report to Arlington the next morning.

'Was it necessary to use such torture on him?' I asked.

'No, bless you, sir,' said the Constable. 'He was confessing before I got the fire properly lit. I just got the irons good and hot to check that he wasn't keeping anything back.'

'And was he?' Arlington enquired.

'I don't think so, My Lord. By the time the poker was glowing, I knew more than his confessor.'

'What did he tell you?'

'He admits that he instigated the attempt to incriminate the Dutch gentleman, though he did not personally do anything in the street. He also says that he can tell us nothing about the murder of the other Dutch gentleman and swore on the souls of several dead relatives that he really knew absolutely nothing about it.'

'And his accomplices? Does he incriminate Paston, for example?'

'He said that Paston was a fervent supporter, My Lord, but he did not admit him to their closer counsels because he thought him unreliable.'

'Unreliable? Why?'

'Because he is stupid, sir. He thought Paston might betray them by accident.'

'Yes, that rings true,' Arlington smiled. 'Were others named?'

'I have a list here, signed by Mr Coleman. I'm afraid the signature is a little shaky, but I couldn't do much about that. The gentleman was fearfully moved, particularly when I ordered his drawers pulled down.'

I could well believe that. I think I would sign any list I was presented with when faced by a torturer with a red-hot poker, even if my drawers were fully up.

Arlington perused the list before handing it to me. 'No one of any account there,' he said. 'But I think we might round them up and take them to the Tower, Constable. See if they know anything about the murder of Mr Wevers. Try not to inflict any lasting damage just in case they are innocent. It is impolitic; hanging a maimed man may excite misplaced sympathy for him.'

I have not seen many executions — strictly, I have seen none, because if I have been near to one I have always closed my eyes at the crucial moments — but I hope I would feel some sympathy for any man about to have his life snuffed out, maimed or otherwise. However, I could understand Arlington's argument.

There were no names on the list that I recognised, so I handed it back to Arlington.

The Constable was dismissed to begin the arrests of the men named. In view of the urgency, it was agreed that this should be done as soon as possible, even if they had to be arrested at night.

'It proves to the miscreants that we mean business,' Arlington explained. 'It is always more terrifying to be arrested at night than in the day.'

If they all proved as pliable as Coleman, it was possible that we should have a goodly number of confessions by bedtime. Purely out of curiosity, I wondered whether each would have his own brazier and poker, or whether one red-hot poker would suffice for all of them, but it seemed unduly inquisitive to ask, so I shall never know.

At my request, Arlington had me conducted to Mr Coventry, who received me very civilly. He dismissed his confidential secretary and instructed that we were not to be disturbed.

'I understand from your questions last evening that you are interested in Mr Morley, Master,' he said.

I thought it best to frame my questions to exclude extraneous matter. 'I am, Mr Coventry, but I do not want to trespass upon the secrets of the realm any further than I must.'

'Thank you,' said Coventry, 'that is helpful. May I ask how Mr Morley came to your notice?'

'Certainly. You will, I think, be aware that one of our party was murdered some days ago. I was informed by Lord Arlington that he was being followed by Mr Morley who, unfortunately, had lost sight of him at the critical moment. I was able to obtain an interview with Mr Morley, who was seated behind a screen and who spoke through Lord Arlington, and who told me that he saw nothing of any value to my investigation. I did not have the opportunity to ask who set him on.'

'And as I indicated last night, I did not know. But I have made enquiries, and I am somewhat wiser. The request to observe Mr Wevers came from the Navy Office.'

'Forgive me, but I must be clear. Did this information come from the Navy Office, or from Mr Morley?'

Coventry permitted himself a small smile. 'Ay, there's the rub! There is no written request, and it was not authorised by any of the competent officials here. I therefore asked Morley why he was following Wevers, and it was he who informed me that it was requested by the Navy Office. It was informal and highly irregular, and I have reminded him that he takes his orders from this department and no other.'

'Did he explain why the Navy Office was suspicious of mijnheer Wevers?'

'Yes, he said that they had been informed that he had been showing interest in the work of His Majesty's dockyards.'

'I see.' I sat for a few moments in silence, then I decided to chance my arm. 'I don't believe him,' I said, 'and you don't either, do you?'

'No,' said Coventry candidly. 'By their nature, spies are unruly men. Like a young stallion they must be curbed at all times, and they know it. Of course, they must use their own initiative on occasion, but I have never known a man in our pay to undertake unauthorised work in this land. Morley could not remember exactly who commissioned him, except that he said he was of the Navy Office. I have made enquiries there, and no-one admits to that act. Indeed, I am assured that no fear of espionage existed, the bulk of the Navy having been moved out of London for the duration of your visit and the guard on the London yards having been strengthened.'

'Thank you for so full an answer,' I said. 'I appreciate your frankness. But perhaps I may presume upon you a little more.

How, then, did the King and Lord Arlington know what Morley had been doing?'

'That intrigued me too,' Coventry confessed. 'My Lord tells me that he was informed of Morley's presence by the Sergeant whose men were summoned by Mr Pepys. When the Sergeant announced that all present were to be taken to the watch house for examination — excepting your party, of course — Mr Morley drew him aside and revealed his identity, saying that Lord Arlington would vouch for him.'

'Lord Arlington? He did not ask for you to be informed?'

'Apparently not; but then, consider that he knew Lord Arlington would be informed of Mr Wevers' death and may have felt that His Lordship would be as able as I would to vouch for him.'

That was true. It may have simply been the easiest way of having himself spared detention for a while; but so far as I knew, nobody who had been at the scene had been detained for long.

I drew myself out of my reverie. 'I am sorry. I am sitting here thinking and wasting your valuable time. This is not my world, Mr Coventry. I do not understand how spies work, and therefore I do not know when they behave in a strange way, since all their actions are strange to me.'

Coventry smiled that curious slight smile of his again. 'Master, I am familiar with the ways of spies, and some of their actions here are strange to me too.'

I hate being unable to comprehend something. I first noticed this when I was at school and struggled to understand geometry, but it has dogged me all my life since then. It exasperates me, particularly when I feel I ought to know it. I recall reading an Anabaptist pamphlet and knowing in my heart that it was complete rubbish without being able to put my finger on exactly why. That same feeling was clouding my thoughts now. For a couple of days I had had the idea that the solution was almost within my grasp, but I could not quite nail it down.

Oh, I knew how the killing had been done. That was trivial. I also knew who had done it, but not why, and until I could show that, I had only my unsupported deduction (and a bit of guesswork) to put before the King. However keen he was to see a guest's murder properly investigated, I doubted he would hang anyone on my word alone, nor should he.

Nevertheless, I was not without options. I could trudge around London a little more with a view to finding out what I could about a couple of people, and I began by asking at the gatehouse for some directions.

When I arrived at Seething Lane, Mr Pepys was at home and immediately received me. He sent at once for some wine and invited me to sit in his office where we would not be disturbed.

'You took quite a chance coming here without notice,' he said. 'Not that I mind, of course, but I am often from home. As it happens, I am today attending to Trinity House business, and it is more convenient to have it brought to me here than to journey out to Deptford.'

'This Deptford,' I asked, 'is it far?'

'Two hours' walk, and that only if you can force your way through the crowds on London Bridge. But I am sure you did not come here to ask me about Deptford, Master.'

'Indeed, no. I was hoping that you could help me with some further information about the night when Wevers was killed. I know the Dutchmen who were there, of course, but I did not perfectly understand who the Englishmen were, and since you assembled the party I hoped you could help me with that.'

'I am not sure that I can, Master. There was Mr Dawkins, of course, who works for me. I've known him for some time. He was a clerk at the Admiralty until last year, when he became a surveyor of lights and a river pilot. Few men know the Thames as well as he does. Then there was Mr Laurel, who is a tutor at a school I have some connection with. Both being unmarried, they were game for a frolic at short notice. And I believe you met Robert Buckie, a gentleman from Scotland.'

'I did not understand how Mr Buckie was employed.'

Pepys laughed. 'Few of us do. I don't think he is. He has a pension from the King for services rendered shortly after the death of the King's father.'

I said nothing, but I may have raised an enquiring eyebrow.

'When the King was hard-pressed, Mr Buckie supplied him with money and horses.'

'He was a rich man, then?'

'No, he was a thief. But His Majesty was not in a position to be too choosy in 1650. Buckie risked his neck on several occasions on His Majesty's behalf.'

'And Captain Hallow?'

'Hallow is a captain of the militia, it seems. I don't know him well, but I have seen him about Whitehall a few times. Dawkins knows him better than I do, though I recall his saying that Hallow invited himself once he knew we were supplied with money, for Dawkins would not have judged him fit company.'

'Did he say why?'

'Only that Hallow sometimes makes himself disagreeable.'

That I could well imagine. The man had a face like a half-sucked prune all evening.

I could think of nothing more useful to ask, so I thanked Mr Pepys for his time and took my leave. I paused to admire the

Tower of London from a very safe distance — knowing what business was carried on there, I did not choose to venture too close — and thought the calm of a church might help me muster my thoughts. I found a fine old church with beautiful carvings very close to Mr Pepys' house and slipped inside.

Since nobody was in sight, I dipped my hand inside my shirt to collect my rosary from the inner pocket and began to say my prayers, expecting to be safe from any interruption. And so I was, until I interrupted myself.

I was about three-quarters of the way through when a thought impressed itself on my brain. Someone inside the palace was pulling the strings.

How did Hallow know that a jaunt was being planned in order to invite himself? Certainly I had seen him around the place, but only at the general audiences. And why did Dawkins permit him to join us unless there was already some acquaintance between them, and, if so, how?

It was likely that the villain Coleman was the person responsible, I decided, and so abandoned my prayers with a muttered apology to God, who must be getting quite used to my sudden interruptions by now.

Not without trepidation I presented myself at the gate of the Tower of London and asked if I might speak to the Constable. After a short while I was conducted within, though I admit that I shuddered just a little as the great gate clattered shut behind me. I watched anxiously to see whose pocket the key went into.

The warder and I climbed some steps and entered at the foot of a building where some stairs took us to a bright chamber. The Constable entered through a door at the rear. I noted with concern that he was wiping his hands vigorously on a cloth.

'Master Mercurius, what brings you here?' he said cheerfully.

I have found that sadists are often cheerful. They whistle happily as they turn the rack or apply the thumbscrews. That, I presume, is because they enjoy their work so much. They must feel it keenly when they have no customers for their trade.

'Is Mr Coleman still here, Constable?'

'As it happens, he is, Master. His Majesty is keen that he should depart the realm as soon as possible, but at the moment he is recovering himself in one of the chambers upstairs.'

'By your leave, may I speak with him? You are very welcome to stay.'

The Constable chuckled. 'Bless you, Master, I think we can trust you not to do him any harm. With his wickedness he's bound for Hell anyway. Nothing you or I can do to him will make any difference to that.'

I was about to launch into a theological argument about the redemptive power of unearned suffering but decided this was not the time or place. I can rarely resist a good argument, but to my credit I bit my tongue and followed the Constable through the back door and up another flight of stairs. There was a guard outside a door who stepped to one side as the Constable unlocked it.

Mr Coleman looked up as he heard the key. To my surprise, he was in quite a good condition physically. There were a few red marks on his wrists and ankles from the ropes that had bound him, and I suspected that under his shirts his ribs were probably a little tender, judging by the hunched position he had adopted and the wince he produced as he tried to stand. The scars, such as they were, were mental. The man was plainly terrified.

'I'll leave the key in the lock on the outside,' the Constable said. 'Sometimes men facing execution have been known to attempt to fling themselves on a warder's halberd to have a quick death, and we can't have that, can we?' He addressed Coleman directly. 'I trust you'll comport yourself as a gentleman and not attempt to pervert this man's mind with your papistry. Just remember that we've warmed the irons to entertain your friends below, and I'll warrant they're still glowing, so you'll be on your best behaviour and answer the gentleman truthfully.'

Coleman nodded. If his eyes had opened any wider, they would have fallen out on his cheeks. It was clear that the sight of the hot irons had made a lasting impression on his memory. 'I had hoped for a Catholic priest to offer consolation, sir,' he croaked.

'I haven't come for any spiritual reason, Mr Coleman,' I replied.

He looked downcast, and I took pity on him. I was taking a great chance, but I could not ignore a soul, even a black one, in torment. Maybe a black one needs consolation even more than a saint's. 'I will take you into my confidence, sir,' I whispered. 'I am secretly a Catholic priest, and before I go I will hear your confession, if you will undertake not to tell anyone my secret.'

Coleman looked doubtful, so I retrieved my breviary from my inner pocket and showed it to him. He grabbed my hand and fervently kissed the breviary. I hope he did not notice as I wiped it on my gown before returning it to its hiding place.

'Forgive me, Father, for I have sinned,' he began.

'You certainly have,' I answered, which is an unusual way for a confession to start, but it seemed justified in the circumstances. 'But that is not what brings you here.'

'I believed, and believe still, that an alliance with France is the best course for my faith and my country,' he said. 'I have, it seems, lost that argument.'

'So it seems. And I understand that you were responsible for the attempt to make out an innocent man to be a thief.'

'I will seek God's forgiveness for that. I thought that if the party were disgraced, it would gain me more time to make my case to the Duke of York and encourage him to deny his daughter's hand to your master.'

'Let us then move on. When that failed, what was your next plan?'

Coleman looked up, appearing astonished. 'I had none, Master. Having no access to the Princesses, I thought perhaps I might seek to influence their stepmother, the Duchess, but she said that she could not counsel them against their father's instruction. And the Duke would not argue with his brother the King.'

'But then you heard of our party and some Englishmen going out into the city. Whom did you tell?'

'Nobody, Master. I did not know of it.'

'You didn't tell Mr Paston, or Captain Hallow, for example?'

'Paston was away in Norfolk. Who is Hallow?'

The man was telling the truth, I was sure of it. I said that I had no further questions for him, and bade him tell me all he wished in an act of confession, which is a secret between a man, his priest and his God.

And that's why I'm not going to tell you what he said.

CHAPTER SEVENTEEN

I was told that half a million people lived in London then, and so far as I could see most of them could have been suspects. Any one of them could have walked up to Wevers in the street and stuck a dagger in him without warning or even a motive; but I was fairly sure that I knew the two people who had combined to make that happen. I lacked any connection between them, even of the most suppositious type, and there was the small difficulty that in one case the evidence steered me away.

I returned to Whitehall, acutely aware that I had missed dinner, and contemplated stopping at an inn or chop house to rectify the loss, but when I arrived at the gate I discovered dinner was still being served, a consequence of the King's highly irregular hours.

I tried to slip in unnoticed but failed dismally, being immediately hailed by His Majesty across the room.

'Ho! Mercurius!'

When His Majesty spoke, all other voices were stilled, of course, so I made my way to the great table and bowed in greeting.

'No ceremony, Mercurius! Come up here and tell me what you've been doing. Arlington, shift along.'

There followed a comic moment as each person in turn to the King's right made the next person move until eventually someone was compelled to shift to another table.

'Your Majesty, I...'

'Get some wine and food first, man. I can recommend the duck.'

'Thank you, sir.'

'And that gammon is excellent.'

'Thank you, sir.'

'And there's a baked pike somewhere.'

'Thank you, sir. I'm well supplied now.'

'Jolly good. Well, let's hear it. Don't dither!'

I explained that I had seen Coventry, Pepys and Coleman and recounted the discussions there just as I have done in these pages.

'You've seen Coleman? How is he?'

'Miserable and frightened, Your Majesty.'

'Excellent. Exactly how I'd want him to feel.'

The Duke of York was not in company with us, but I doubt Charles would have said anything different if he had been.

'My brother knows I mean business this time. There'll be no more dismissing a man then finding him another post in his household. Isn't that right, Arlington?'

'Indeed so, Your Majesty,' Arlington said.

I took the opportunity to ask my next question in front of the King, which I thought might help me to get a truthful answer from Arlington. 'Might I have another interview with Morley?'

Arlington looked uncomfortable. 'He has been allowed to leave,' he said.

'Why do you want to talk to him?' asked Charles.

'Because he is the leading suspect in the murder of Wevers. He was, after all, the last person we know who, by his own admission, saw Wevers alive.'

Charles chewed slowly on a chicken leg. 'He's right there, you know, Arlington. Why did you let Morley go, eh?'

'Because you ord—… I will see if we can find him again,' Arlington replied. 'At least we know where he will be when his salary is next due.'

'Where's that?' I asked.

'Why, at the Treasury Chambers,' Arlington replied. 'They're behind the King's laboratory where you were the other day. All the King's servants are paid there.'

'May I ask when they are paid?' I enquired.

'It varies. I approve the list by the third Sunday of the month, then they are paid on different days according to their employment to ease the workload of the treasury. So, for example, the gardeners and masons attend on Monday, the household staff on Wednesday, and so on.'

We would have left before the next pay-day, but at least I could leave a request for his arrest, I supposed. Fortunately, the King, who was much more highly regarded than I was, had a better idea.

'Arlington, you must know how to find him, in case we have a job for him.'

'I don't, Your Majesty, but Mr Coventry will.'

Coventry was two places to the left of the King, so he was summoned to move one place closer.

'Coventry, I want you to get a summons to that fellow Morley to present himself here to Mercurius.'

'Your Majesty, if his appearance becomes known, it renders him useless to us.'

'I know that, Coventry, but if the man is a murderer he's useless to us anyway, because he'll be dangling from a gallows.'

'Perhaps if Master Mercurius were to give us a list of questions, we could ask on his behalf,' Coventry said.

'I'm afraid it's his appearance that matters to me. I want to know if people recognise him,' I answered.

'Well, that's plain enough, Coventry. Get the man here. He can meet Mercurius in private somewhere. Mercurius, you'll undertake not to share any information about him if he's not the murderer, won't you?'

'Yes, Your Majesty.'

I thought that clinched matters, but Arlington was still vexed at having a spy unmasked. Judging by their performance during our recent war with England, perhaps he did not have many good ones.

'May I make an alternative suggestion, Your Majesty? If we were to bring Morley into this hall, Mercurius' witnesses could observe the crowd and tell us if they recognise anyone. That way, if they don't, his appearance will not be revealed.'

Charles sighed. 'I don't mind how the thing is done, Arlington. Just have it performed so that Master Mercurius may complete his investigation.'

It was clear that we were coming very close to the end of the King's attention span, so I dropped the subject. 'Thank you, Your Majesty,' I said.

'You may leave us, Mercurius.'

I was not sure whether the normal etiquette was to take your half-eaten pasty with you or not, but it seemed unhygienic to leave it, so I kept it in my hands, rose and bowed. It was difficult to see where I was going to sit, because in the wake of my removal a lot of people shuffled along a place or moved from one table to another, but Van Langenburg caught my eye and indicated a seat opposite him.

'Now you can tell me what you told the King,' he smiled crookedly, 'if you have no objection to speaking to the head of your delegation.'

'Your pardon,' I quickly replied. It would not do to fall out with him, especially if I had to return to The Hague with my tail between my legs and an incomplete enquiry. Who knew what he would tell William? I would probably finish up as a village schoolmaster in one of the West Frisian Islands, if there was one small enough to humiliate me adequately.

I hastened to explain to Van Langenburg what I had discovered. If all went well, I might be able to conclude my enquiry on the morrow whenever Morley showed up.

'If only Arlington and the King had allowed me to interview Morley in person earlier instead of conducting that ridiculous charade, I might already have finished,' I said.

Van Langenburg said something, but I did not hear it. My head was full of little bells indicating that the whole thing was suddenly clear.

I could not wait to get to my room and write out my argument so that I could be sure I had it straight in my head. Sometimes when I was teaching I liked to quote Proverbs, chapter nine, verse nine: "Give instruction to the wise and they will become wiser still", but just at that moment another verse from Proverbs, chapter twelve, verse fifteen, was leaping out at me: "Fools think their own way is right, but the wise listen to advice."

There was still one stumbling block, the one piece of evidence I needed to complete the chain. I needed a reason why someone would kill Wevers, and I could not think of one. I could think of plenty of reasons why others would do it, but not the person I believed must have done it. I had to discover that before I saw Morley, because then I planned to reveal all in a masterpiece of theatre. Not, you understand, because I was vain and wanted the applause of the audience, but because revealing the killer was going to be a lot safer in a large crowd with plenty of armed guards on hand. I had no doubt that he would kill me to silence me if he had to.

I could not sleep and struggled to keep my mind on any other work, so I said my prayers and then busied myself packing my chest for the journey home which, God willing, would come in a day or so. I was quite prepared to go and sit on the quay all night if it brought it any closer. I would even load the ship myself. It's not that I did not know that I loved my homeland so much, but I had come to find England hateful to me.

CHAPTER EIGHTEEN

The sun rose, and so did I. To the astonishment of the priest, I was in the chapel when he arrived for the first office of the day, and I breakfasted with some of the court officials and absolutely none of the courtiers or Dutch guests. So far as I know, King Charles had just gone to bed after an evening at the theatre. There was no play being performed, but he did not seem to find this an obstacle to his preferred type of entertainment.

As soon as I had eaten, I positioned myself in the Privy Garden and waited for the clerks to open the Treasury Chambers. I could not see the doors, you understand, because these rooms were at the rear of the building with access only from inside, but I could see the guards move into place whose purpose was to stop anyone attempting to make off with the King's money.

The clerks looked up as I entered the counting house.

'We're not open for the Chapel staff today,' said one with the maximum of disinterest.

'Good, because I'm not one of them,' I replied.

The clerk was taking more interest in me now. 'Ah, you're one of the foreign gentlemen.'

'I am Master Mercurius of the University of Leiden,' I introduced myself, 'and His Majesty has given me permission to examine your records.'

'He hasn't told us,' the other clerk at the table replied.

'Does His Majesty speak to you often?' I asked.

I had not anticipated this obstruction and was kicking myself that I had not obtained a letter from the King, or Arlington, or Coventry, or whoever would impress them.

'He's got a point there,' the first clerk decided. 'What did you want to see, sir?'

'The payment records for the Royal Household, please.'

'For how long?'

'Let's start with the latest and work backwards,' I said.

The clerk opened a large book and turned it towards me. I ran my finger slowly down the list of names. As is often the case when I am researching, my mind was distracted by matters that seemed much more interesting than those I was supposed to be looking for. For example, I was shocked to discover that Charles paid his gardener nearly as much as I got from the University. *Perhaps I should consider a change of career*, I thought, though I had never been comfortable in the company of worms.

There were a lot of people employed there, and I was three-quarters of the way down the fourth page when I found what I wanted. I asked the clerks to find the comparable entry for previous months. It did not take long, and within a quarter of an hour I knew who had killed Wevers. I also had an idea why, and — without wishing to fall into the sin of pride — I was delighted that my revelation of the night before was correct. Now all I had to do was wait for Arlington's men to bring Morley in.

With nothing more useful to do for the rest of the day, I decided to pay a farewell visit to mijnheer Biscop at the Dutch church, so I asked the clerks to give me directions to Austin Friars. It was a fine morning with no threat of rain, so I set out with, as they say, a spring in my step and the keen anticipation of the King's satisfaction at my work; and if the King was satisfied, William would be satisfied too. And that was what really concerned me, because William had it in his power to make my life miserable. One cloud upon the horizon was the suggestion from Mary that I might be her chaplain in The Hague when she was married. I would have to sidestep that particular threat somehow by, for example, forgetting all the English I had so painstakingly learned. If that didn't work, I could try making a lewd remark to one of her ladies-in-waiting, if I knew any such language, which I didn't, but I could always ask the students in Leiden for some tips.

My route out to the east took me past the Stocks Market, where a deal of produce of all kinds was sold, and where I saw a statue of King Charles mounted upon a horse trampling some poor fellow. I wove my way in and out of the stalls, looking to see what was to be had. It was mainly meat and fish, but also some herbs and vegetables. I sauntered there listening to the noise and enjoying the business, and then I returned to the statue. Some passing fellow told me the man was Oliver Cromwell, in which event I assumed the statue was allegorical, as it assuredly never happened like that, though it would probably not be wise to say so to the King.

The market continued around the corner in Poultry, which was aptly named, since it was filled with chickens and ducks in baskets and cages. I walked in and out of the stalls, and stepped back into an alleyway to allow a cart to pass.

And that was when someone threw a sack over my head and knocked me off my feet.

I cannot narrate much about what may have happened after that until I woke up to find myself tied to a chair in an upstairs room somewhere. The sack had been removed but I was blindfolded. I guessed it to be upstairs because the street noise seemed to be below me.

'Would you like a drink?' a man asked. I knew the voice but could not put a face to it.

'Yes, please,' I said, 'then I'd like to go home.'

'Unfortunately, that won't be possible for a while. If you weren't a man of God you'd be dead by now, but I can't kill a minister.'

'I'm very pleased to hear that.' I almost told him I was a man of God twice over in case it made me even safer, but I decided I could not rely on him to keep my secret.

'So I intend to keep you here long enough to make my escape. A day should suffice, by which time I shall have disappeared from view. It's sad that I shall have to find a new occupation, but I doubt that the powers that be will want to employ me once you have spoken to them.'

'They won't need me to speak to them. They know what I was thinking.'

'Ah, if only that were true! But you see, I did a little snouting around last night and nobody knew what you were thinking. So, you see, if you can't tell them I won't be under suspicion.'

This was ominous. If I were in his position and wanted to escape a nasty death on the scaffold with the tantalising little extras that rulers like to throw in these days, I would kill me on the spot. Given a choice between killing one person and dying and killing two and getting away, the rational man has only one option. I decided to play for time. 'I assume that your kidnapping of me is a confession of guilt,' I said, 'but what exactly would you like to confess to?'

He laughed. 'Nothing at all. But I'll tell you one thing I didn't do. I didn't kill Wevers.'

'I know,' I said. 'I'd worked that out. In a strict sense, you didn't. But you know who did, and you set them to it.'

'Careful, Mr Minister. I might not kill you, but I didn't say I wouldn't hurt you.'

'Are you a Catholic?'

'No!' he said scornfully. 'I belong to the Church of England. Why?'

'Oh, no reason,' I lied. If he had been a Catholic, I might have tried suggesting that harming a priest is a mortal sin. Though, given what he had already done, I don't suppose he would have lost too much sleep about it.

I heard a bell striking the hour. It was eleven o'clock, so I must have been knocked out for almost an hour. I was hoping it had been a bit longer so we would all be going to bed soon, when I could do some thinking and praying; mainly praying, because I could not see a way out of this on my own. Having said that, I had been praying for some divine help for a few days, and it was clear that my petitions were not getting to the top of God's daily list.

I tried listening hard to see if I could get some clue to where I was. There was some street noise, but I could not hear any clear speech. It would have been really helpful if someone had asked which was the nearest church, for example.

Have you ever noticed that when things happen suddenly, you have difficulty sorting them into the right order in your own mind? On top of that, I could not see anything, so all I heard was noises, but suddenly there was a loud, close bang and a draught of cold air which led me to think that someone had opened the door. A number of feet could be heard running in, but they stopped some distance away.

'Stay back!' shouted my kidnapper, and it was clear from the retreating shuffle that they took his command seriously, whoever they were. There was some murmuring, then another set of feet coming up the stairs.

'Don't be a fool,' someone said. 'Put that knife down.'

That explained why everyone was very happy to stay back.

'If you harm Master Mercurius, I'll see to it that your execution is extremely drawn out,' said the newcomer, whose voice I had just recognised. It was Samuel Pepys.

I need hardly add that the most pressing thought in my mind at that moment was that the promise of a slow, lingering death for my murderer was no consolation to me, but you have to make some allowance for the novelty of the situation in which Pepys found himself.

I realise that I have never given a description of myself in these journals, and I do not propose to do so now, but I have to explain that I have quite a high bridge to my nose. [No, Van der Meer, I do not have an unusually large nose; I have a normal sized nose on a delicately featured face. Such impudence in a clerk! There are plenty of people who would like your job. Yes, even at these wages.]

Anyway, I could not see anything through the blindfold looking forward; but I could see a little underneath the blindfold looking down towards my chin. And what I could see was a right hand holding a narrow-bladed knife in front of my throat. He plainly had in mind cutting my throat with a great sweep since the end of the blade must have been somewhere near my left ear.

Desperation makes a man do some strange things, so I said a silent prayer and then sank my teeth deep into the base of the thumb and held on for dear life. There was a deal of screaming and yelling, and some scuffling and buffeting, and suddenly my chair was tipped over violently. Some kind person pulled the blindfold off — they might have undone the knot first — and once my eyes became accustomed to the light, I could see about four men lying on top of someone on the floor, while Pepys was standing over me with a smile playing loosely across his features.

'You had us worried for a while there, Master,' he said.

'I was worried myself, Mr Pepys,' I replied. 'I don't suppose somebody could cut my bonds?'

Pepys looked around for the dropped knife, found it across the room, and began sawing at the ropes. 'Is that your blood around your mouth, or his?' he asked solicitously.

'I don't know,' I admitted. 'I just knew that if I bit his hand, he could not use the knife on me.'

Pepys nodded. 'He could have transferred the knife to his other hand,' he said.

I think I went pale. 'I never thought of that,' I admitted.

'It is your good fortune that he didn't either.'

One of his men began cutting the rope from my feet. My wrists and ankles were sore, and my legs were like marzipan, but God be praised I was unharmed. Pepys helped me to my feet and I dusted myself down.

'I assume we're taking him back to Whitehall?' Pepys asked.

'Yes, please,' I said.

As I had expected, I found myself looking at the angry face of Captain Hallow.

CHAPTER NINETEEN

I had a more comfortable journey to Whitehall than Hallow did. Since he was unable to walk by virtue of having his legs strapped together, he was picked up and dumped on a cart borrowed from one of the market traders. I, meanwhile, was invited to repair to the carriage which had brought Mr Pepys thither.

'I am grateful for your timely intervention, but how did you know where I was?' I asked.

'Ah, there you may thank some public-spirited citizens. A couple of them noticed some ruffians throwing a sack over your head. One ran for the watch, while the other followed the miscreants at a distance. The watch came for me when a witness said that he had been speaking to you about a statue. They were struck by his description of you as a "German minister of God" and, knowing that we had been in company on the night that Wevers died, it crossed someone's mind that it might be you.'

This is the point at which I express gratitude to the English for being a nosy people. In the Low Countries, people would probably have thought that if I want to have a sack thrown over my head, it is none of their business.

'I came to the market as fast as I could, and we were informed that you had been taken along Old Jewry into Coleman Street. There the pursuer had lost sight of you, but he assumed you must be near because nobody he asked further along the street had seen you. Thus when we arrived we had only a couple of dozen houses to examine. But our search was helped by a keen-eyed woman who wondered why a hanging had been put across one of the upstairs windows of a house opposite her own. One of my men crept up the stairs and listened at the door, and the rest you know.'

Our arrival at the gates of Whitehall occasioned some interest, with even more evidenced when the cart bearing Hallow arrived some minutes later. Hallow looked rather dishevelled, the result, according to the guards, of an escape attempt when he had rolled off the back of the cart near Blackfriars and attempted to hop into the river. Hallow's account was that through their negligence he had been allowed to fall off the cart and he was merely trying to get out of the carriageway before he was run down.

Arlington had been advised of the commotion and had run to inform the King, with the result that Hallow was ordered to be taken at once to the large chamber where public audiences took place. The King, we were told, was being dressed with haste.

Haste is, of course, a relative term, and it was about half an hour before His Majesty was satisfied with his appearance and joined us. Hallow had been untied except for his wrists and was standing at the foot of the steps to the dais with two guards with swords drawn beside him. As an extra precaution a noose had been looped over his head, and a third guard was standing with his hands on the knot ready to tighten it at a moment's notice.

King Charles noticed this at once. 'That noose will save time, you blackguard! What have you to say for yourself before we hang you?'

Hallow was remarkably composed. 'I humbly say, Your Majesty, that as an Englishman I am entitled to a trial by my peers; and that no evidence has been produced against me; and that, therefore, trusting in Your Majesty's Coronation promise to uphold the law of England, I apprehend no danger of summary judgment and execution.'

'A pretty speech, my fellow. But being blameless may not save you from execution. I speak as one whose father suffered though without stain on his character.'

I grant that there are historians who would dispute that description of King Charles the First, but that was not the time or place to do so, and we all let the remark go uncontested.

Arlington whispered something into His Majesty's ear.

'Is he, by God?' said Charles. 'Well, Master Mercurius, the floor is yours. Explain to us why you bring this man for judgment.'

'Gladly, Your Majesty. But I believe that he has an accomplice, and I am keen that they should not escape. May I have them brought here?'

'Please do,' boomed Charles.

I gave orders to a couple of servants, who rushed off. I have to say that at that moment Charles looked every inch what I expected a king to be. His voice was loud and firm, his presence magnificent, and he stayed awake all through my explanation without more than the occasional sign of boredom, which, I think, is more than some rulers might have done.

I asked for a cup of wine to wet my throat, took a sip, and began my explanation.

'I do not believe in coincidence,' I said. 'And the death of mijnheer Wevers was no street altercation or vulgar robbery. This was a cold-blooded, efficient killing. To bring guilt home to the perpetrator, I have to show that they were in the right place, at the right time, and, if possible, demonstrate a reason for the murder. I believe I can now do all these things.'

There was an appreciative gasp from my audience.

'First, let me tell you what the motive was not. I have had an interview with Edward Coleman. He admits that he was responsible for the attempt to blame mijnheer Preuveneers for the robbery of the silver, but says that he had no part in the murder of Wevers. I believe him, because he made a very frank confession of his misdoings but denied that one vehemently, and because there is someone with a better reason for committing the crime.' I looked to Arlington. 'My Lord Arlington was with me when we examined the chest belonging to Wevers. It contained a secret compartment.'

There was another gasp. This was, it seemed, even better entertainment than the theatre, but that may have been only because it had not cost them a shilling to get in.

'In this compartment we found a handgun and a letter which commanded Wevers to deliver a pouch of money to an Englishman with the alias of Delphi who had provided useful intelligence to the United Provinces during the late war. The pouch was not there, so we may suppose that Wevers had it on him when we went out on his last walk. And since it was not on him when his body was found, we may suppose that the murderer took it. They had very little time to do so, and they did not find the dagger in Wevers' sleeve, so we must assume their search was not thorough. They found the pouch because they were looking for it, and only for that. We cannot know until we find the pouch, but I suspect that they feared that it might contain information they would have found awkward or embarrassing if it fell into the wrong hands. Or, as we would say, the right hands.'

Charles chuckled. He clearly knew his were the right hands.

'It does my country no credit that this episode demonstrates that we employ English spies,' I continued, 'but I can only tell you the truth. And now we come to a key piece of information, because Wevers' instructions told him to ask Delphi some questions about the large ships the English navy was building on the Medway. But it also revealed that the supply of information had dried up over the last six months. I can think of three possibilities for that. One is that Delphi was dead. The second is that he had decided no longer to play the spy. And the third is that he was no longer in a position to supply the information.'

I could see by the look on Pepys' face that he knew what was coming next.

'I thought that the likeliest reason was that Delphi was a naval officer and was now at sea, but there is an objection to that idea which I will come to in a moment. The alternative was that Delphi had worked in the Admiralty but had now taken on a new post. I imagine that this Delphi had need of ready money. It is expensive to live in London, and the salary of an Admiralty clerk is not great.

'The possible objection to Delphi being at sea lurks in the way that Wevers had to make his appointment. It seems that Delphi did not submit his information directly to my country, because whoever gave Wevers his instructions was not able to contact Delphi directly. He had to go via an intermediary, whom I will call Apollo. Wevers was told that Apollo had been commanded to get Delphi to contact him to arrange a rendezvous at which Wevers would pay him for past services and ask for the information about the new ships that I have mentioned. And I assume that such an appointment was made, which Wevers was on his way to keep. Lord Arlington has suggested that it may have been at the Savoy, which was an area where English and Dutch people could mix without drawing attention to themselves, but it does not really matter exactly where it was. The main thing is that the murderer could make a good guess at the route that someone who did not know London well would take, and that he knew when the meeting was planned. Lord Arlington, do you agree with my account thus far?'

'It is as you say,' Arlington agreed.

'The obvious conclusion was that only two people knew of the appointment — Wevers and Delphi. And Delphi was therefore the killer. This was my line of thought for a long time. But then I realised that there was another alternative. We know that Apollo was ordered to get Delphi to make an appointment; but suppose that Apollo did not, or could not do so. Could he have made the appointment himself, without the knowledge of Delphi? In which event it was still true that only two people knew of the appointment, but this time they would be Wevers and Apollo. In fact, we only have Apollo's word for it that Delphi even exists.'

I glanced around the hall to see whether anyone was unsurprised by this suggestion and saw Paston frowning deeply. It was clear that I had lost him in my argument, probably around the time I mentioned the secret compartment.

'I assume that the information provided was found to be good and accurate, or we would not have paid for it and requested more, but perhaps Apollo was just as able to provide it.'

'A moment, Master,' Charles interrupted. 'If there isn't a Delphi, then this fellow is both a spy and a murderer, and we'll only have one execution rather than two. Admittedly it'll be a drawn-out affair, but only one. This is going to be a bit of a puzzle, Arlington. Either we hang him as a naval spy at Execution Dock, or we hang, draw and quarter him at Tyburn, but we can't do both. Or can we?'

Arlington was eager not to allow my explication to be interrupted. 'Perhaps we might address Your Majesty's question when we have heard the whole of what Mercurius has to say,' he suggested.

'What? Oh, yes, of course. Carry on, Master,' said Charles.

'Thank you, Your Majesty,' I replied with a small bow. I do not mind saying that my thoughts had been disrupted by mention of execution. I do not like to think of my efforts leading to the death of a man, particularly a slow and gruesome one. As we had arrived on our first day we had sailed past Execution Dock and seen someone hanging there. The gallows were at the waterline, and we were told that the condemned man was left hanging until the tide had washed over him three times. You just had to hope that the rope had done its job before the tide rose for the first time, because I could not imagine the terror of hanging there as the water reached your chin.

I shook myself out of this line of thought and continued. 'We now come to the matter of Mr Morley. I have to explain to the gentlemen here that Mr Morley is an English spy. I believe Morley to be a pseudonym because the practice in such circles is to use noms de guerre to increase secrecy about their work. I was reliably informed that when Wevers left this place to go to his final appointment he was being followed discreetly by Morley, but that Wevers realised this and was able to slip away using an old trick of entering an inn and hiding behind the door, exiting behind Morley's back when Morley opened the door and entered. I visited the inn at which this manoeuvre was said to have happened. Well, it might; but only if Morley was such an incompetent bungler that a man might escape from him in his wardrobe.'

There was general laughter, led by the King.

'The inn was very small, you see, and it would be very difficult for Morley not to see at a glance from the doorway whether Wevers was there or no. He would never need to go right inside. Thus, it seemed to me that Morley's account was questionable; but since this impugns his professionalism, we have to ask why Morley would give a report that shows himself in such a bad light. Unless, I suppose, he wanted to avoid a graver accusation. And here I note that this ridiculous account serves as Morley's proof of his whereabouts for the time when Wevers was killed. Morley, by his description of events, could not have killed Wevers because he was still looking for him in a place where Wevers was not.'

'That is supposing that Wevers met his death as soon as the party divided,' Arlington interrupted.

'Indeed. But Mr Pepys will agree that when we found Wevers, his body was quite cold. He had not been killed shortly before. One day, perhaps, we will be able to fix the time of death by knowing the temperature of the body. All we can say now is that he was not freshly killed when found. I note also that if he had been killed nearer to nine o'clock, Morley would have furnished himself with proof that he was elsewhere at that time.'

Pepys stepped forward to agree with what had been said, then spoke briefly with Coventry, who called a servant to him and gave him some instructions.

'I have now to thank mijnheer Vlisser for drawing my attention to a detailed map of London on which I was able to see the site of the discovery of the body and which suggested one reason why the inn might have been mentioned. The party divided into two at St Martin-in-the-Fields. One part went with Mr Laurel; I was of that party. The other followed Mr Dawkins to an inn known as The White Cat. I believe that Wevers was part of this group, but that he hung back so that his eventual departure to keep his appointment would not be noticed.

'The alleyway where the body of Wevers was found is a dead end. Nobody would pass through it on the way to anywhere else. But the small inn where Morley claims to have lost touch with Wevers backs onto that lane; and so does The White Cat. Both use the alleyway to access their back doors by which they receive supplies. When you walk along it, you can quite easily tell which gate leads to each inn. I said that nobody would walk along the alleyway; but that does not mean that nobody would walk across it. Your Majesty, Morley entered the small inn at the front, left via the rear door, crossed the alleyway and went in the rear door of The White Cat. Since that is a direct route, he was able to get there around the same time as Mr Dawkins' party and was not missed. If anyone saw him enter the inn from the rear, he might tell them he had been using the privy. And I will claim that the reason Morley mentioned the inn is that he thought someone might have seen him go in there. If we had looked, any of Mr Laurel's party would have had a clear view of it. I will argue that Morley needed that direct route to buy him the time he needed to kill Wevers; or, rather, to have him killed.'

'One moment, Master. Are you saying that Morley had rejoined the party when the body was discovered?' asked Charles.

'Yes, Your Majesty. He was with us.'

'But he did not actually kill Wevers?'

'No, Your Majesty. If he had done so, he could hardly have avoided being spattered with blood. His accomplice stabbed Wevers and then melted away into the crowd by a means I will describe shortly. But first I want to investigate a little more who this Morley is.

'Your Majesty will recall that I asked to speak to Morley and was told that it was not possible. I found this strange, because I had myself heard Your Majesty order him to be detained for his dereliction of duty. I persisted, and I was granted an interview of a kind, but a strange one. I could not see Morley, who was sitting behind a screen; nor could I hear him, because his answers were whispered to Lord Arlington, who then voiced them aloud. Among these questions was one which asked whether Morley had ever been to my country; he asked Lord Arlington what the answer was. Why? Surely a man knows where he has been? But if he were impersonating another man, then he might not. And so I deduced.

'I was wrong, of course. He knew whether he had been, but he did not know whether he should admit that he had been there in the persona of Morley. Anyway, I became convinced that for some reason Lord Arlington was attempting to frustrate my enquiries and that an impostor had been substituted for Morley. And I was even more convinced when the interview ended and I ran out to the garden and looked in through the window, because I could see then that the person behind the screen was none other than Captain Hallow.'

Charles looked sharply at Arlington as if to say that he had bungled badly in allowing that to happen.

'This was a considerable annoyance to me, as you may well imagine,' I continued. 'How could I complete my investigation if the very person charged by Your Majesty with assisting me was impeding my search for the truth? I stopped sharing my discoveries freely with His Lordship, fearing that he would put new obstacles in my path. I despaired of bringing my efforts to a successful conclusion. But I have come to realise that I was mistaken. What possible motive could Lord Arlington have for interfering with my enquiry, particularly because he would be defying Your Majesty in doing so?'

Charles nodded enthusiastically as if it was completely unthinkable that Arlington would do a thing like that. Kings expect to be obeyed; they do not anticipate that their trusted ministers should do otherwise. Arlington simply looked relieved that I was not going to allege malfeasance against him.

'But if there was no deception,' I said, 'then I could see only one conclusion. Captain Hallow and Morley were the same man. And I see from Lord Arlington's face that this is indeed so.'

'God's wounds!' exclaimed the King. 'Is it, Arlington?'

'It is, Your Majesty,' Arlington replied. He had the look of a man who would much rather be tending to his garden at Euston, and expected shortly to be doing just that. All day, every day.

'Well, why didn't you say so, man?' thundered Charles.

'I did not know that there was any suspicion attached to him, Your Majesty. I thought he was only wanted as a witness, but if his identity were revealed, as it now has been, he is of no further use to us.'

Charles was not accustomed to whispering, and as a result he did not do it very well, so when he tried I could hear him quite clearly. 'Have we paid him a lot?'

'Above a hundred pounds a year, Your Majesty, I believe.'

Charles shrugged. 'At least there'll be a saving there,' he muttered.

I waited for permission to continue.

'Are you done, Master?' Charles asked.

'Not quite, Your Majesty. I have three more things to treat of.'

'Dear God,' murmured Charles. 'It's longer than one of Compton's sermons.' He waved to me to continue.

'Those three matters are these. Who was the accomplice? Who is Delphi? And why would Hallow want to kill Wevers anyway? We have already heard that Hallow was employed by this country as a spy, but he was also taking money from my country. I expect that if Mr Coventry had known that, his employment here would have ceased. After all, a man cannot serve two masters.'

'Ha!' cried Charles, suddenly sitting upright. 'That's in the Bible, isn't it?'

'Your Majesty is well instructed,' I said, and I meant it. Many of my undergraduates would not have recognised a quote from Matthew chapter six, verse twenty-four. "No man can serve two masters: for either he will hate the one, and love the other; or else he will hold to the one, and despise the other."

'But why should this become known?' I asked. 'Wevers did not know who Hallow was. He knew of Apollo and Delphi, perhaps, but not their identities. He would inevitably discover who Delphi was if they met, but he need never have found out about Apollo.

'I said earlier that I was not convinced that Delphi existed. Perhaps Hallow had invented him and was pocketing the fees paid to both Delphi and Apollo, but then why complicate the picture by concocting such a person?' I looked around and saw that the man I wanted had been found and was standing at the back under guard. 'Then it became clear to me. There is a man here whose character has been under a shadow, and I hope to lift it. The obvious suspect for the identity of Delphi was a man who previously worked for the Admiralty but who, a few months past, moved to a new post at Trinity House. Is that not so, Mr Dawkins?'

Dawkins attempted to rush forward but was stopped by a blow from a guard's truncheon which dropped him to the floor.

'Pray do not hurt him!' I exclaimed. 'He is not such a villain as I thought. It is true that Dawkins supplied the information that Hallow sold to my country. But he did so not as a traitor, but in the belief that Hallow was authorised to have it as a Captain of militia. He used his military commission to go places where others could not go. Having gained the trust of Dawkins, he interrogated him for the information he retailed. Dawkins may, perhaps, have been too trusting; but he was not wicked.'

'That's a matter of opinion,' growled Charles.

'The point here, Your Majesty, is twofold. First, Dawkins could not unwittingly supply any more information of interest to Hallow now that he had changed employment; and Hallow could see the payments from the United Provinces ending. He needed that money to live the life he wanted, particularly to pay his gambling debts. But if he allowed Wevers to meet Dawkins, Wevers would discover that Dawkins had never thought that he was a spy and that no more information would be forthcoming. Hallow therefore arranged a rendezvous that purported to come from Dawkins, but was actually an appointment with death that he proposed to keep. And he arranged for his agent in this palace to slip it under Wevers' door.'

I was rewarded with another gasp.

Charles was indignant. With his heavy black eyebrows he was particularly good at being indignant. 'There has been someone here working for this scoundrel!'

'There has, Your Majesty.'

'Name the man!'

'By your leave, sir, let me first explain how they were identified. Many of us are people of habit. We do the same things in the same way day by day; so when someone does something different, we wonder why. When we came here, Wevers and I were assigned the services of a young maid called Meg. She had not been here long, a fact which was verified by Mrs Paston. Now, we men do not generally notice female servants.'

'Oh, I don't know about that,' grinned Charles.

'Leaving that aside,' I said, not a little flustered, 'we do not usually notice who serves us. But women do. They have much more to do with them, so if Mrs Paston did not recognise Meg, we may assume that she was newly arrived. So I went to the Treasury to ascertain when she first came, and I found that she came into service just two weeks before our party arrived. As one of the junior maids, she was assigned to the junior members of the party, Wevers and myself. It was a lucky chance that she was given Wevers to attend to, but she could have worked her mischief even if she was not, once she had been admitted to the building. With leave to go into Wevers' chamber, she was able to search for anything that incriminated Hallow, though she seems not to have discovered the secret compartment in the chest. I found Meg in my room looking through papers, but she passed it off as tidying. But that was not her most suspicious action.'

Charles interrupted. 'Master Mercurius, have you a deal more to say? For if you have, for God's sake go away and write a book about it.'

'Not much more, Your Majesty. I noted that on the morning after Wevers died, the laundry was taken from my room in the usual way. But when I looked in Wevers' room, his laundry was still there. His bed did not need making, because he had not slept in it, but at the time when I looked in it was not generally known that Wevers was dead. So why had Meg taken my laundry, but not Wevers', unless, I suppose, she knew that he would not have need of laundry any longer? How did she know he was dead before others did?

'Then at the banquet I noticed another unusual matter. With so many candles and the fire blazing, it was a very warm evening. The servants went about their business with their sleeves rolled up and, where possible, their shirts unfastened at the neck. Yet Meg was serving me wearing a large, old-fashioned collar. It covered her like a shawl. But she needed to, you see, because she only has one serving dress, like most of the servants here. And it had been splashed on her right shoulder with Wevers' blood when she stabbed him.'

The gasps I had received earlier were nothing compared with what I heard now.

'When we arrived, she made overtures of a very familiar nature to both myself and Wevers and was rebuffed. I do not think that they were genuine, certainly not in my case. She wished to give that impression. And I believe that she was lying in wait for Wevers by that alleyway. When he came towards her, she stepped out and made to kiss him. He may have tried to avoid the unwanted kiss, but he did not see the dagger she plunged into his breast. She gripped him tightly to her, disguising her true action, and then Hallow stepped forward and together they took Wevers into the alleyway and left him there. No doubt she was able to pin him upright against the wall or a fence while Hallow searched him and retrieved the purse. To a passer-by she would look like a whore with a client.

'Then, when they were done, she removed the dagger and let him fall to the ground. Blood might dribble when the dagger was removed, but they had stepped to one side so that she was only slightly spattered at that point because the heart was not beating any longer. And finally she wrapped herself in her cloak to conceal the blood on her dress and went off to clean herself while Hallow continued to The White Cat to establish that he had been there all along. I think that perhaps that company was too rowdy and he feared that they might not recall his presence, so he later came to join Mr Laurel's group and took a little wine with us.

'It was Meg who stole Vlisser's dagger; Meg who told Hallow of the planned entertainments; and Meg who took Wevers' New Testament. She may have thought it was the codebook that Lord Arlington and I found; the two were similar in appearance, and since the Testament is in Dutch, Meg could not read it.'

Charles rose to his feet. 'Is this woman here?'

The guards I had dispatched earlier dragged Meg forward.

'What have you to say for yourself?'

Meg began to cry and simply shook her head. Arlington stepped forward with a candle and lifted her collar.

'There are stains here, Your Majesty, just as the Master described.'

Meg pulled away from the candle's flame.

'That's not the worst flame you'll face, my girl!' said Charles.

His words had the most terrible effect upon Meg, who screamed for mercy.

'I can hang a man, but 'twere indecent to raise a woman in skirts up,' said Charles. 'Aiding a foreign agent can only be treason, the sentence whereof is to be burned alive at the stake.'

Meg threw herself on the floor, racked with sobs.

'If I may, Your Majesty,' I said, 'I may bring forward one reason for mercy. I decided early that Meg had done the stabbing, but I did not know why. Then, when I saw the pay records of the court, it became clear. This is Meg Hallow; Captain Hallow is her brother.'

'What!' bellowed Charles, and turning to Hallow, asked, 'You villain, is this true?'

'It is, Your Majesty,' Hallow said.

'He told me that the Dutch gentleman was a spy,' said Meg, who no longer sounded quite as common as heretofore. 'In killing him, we were protecting this Kingdom.'

'You should have known better than to trust the word of such a blackguard,' pronounced Charles. 'Whatever he claimed, you deliberately compassed the death of a man, and that's murder. You won't burn alive, perhaps, being strangled before the flames are lit, but you'll still burn.'

Arlington bent over to whisper in the royal ear.

'What? Oh, I suppose so,' Charles murmured. 'That's all a matter for the judges to decide, and I shan't influence them. But if they condemn you, don't expect clemency from me.'

I stood despondent. My work was done, and it was to cost a man and a woman their lives; but that would not bring poor Wevers back to us.

'Take them away,' ordered Charles. 'Master Mercurius, you have told a curious tale, and have earned our thanks for your diligence and intelligence in opening this mystery to us. But now I think we must quit this hall and attend to happier things. Let us all retire for an hour while refreshments are made ready. Master, I would speak to you in private.'

I bowed and made to follow.

'Wait here ten minutes,' said Charles. 'After so long a discourse on your part, I badly need to use the privy.'

CHAPTER TWENTY

When I was admitted to Charles' presence, he had removed his wig and was sitting with his feet in a bowl of perfumed water. 'I feel a gout coming on,' he explained. 'And I am weary of spirit. Such treachery beneath my very nose! I am surprised that my ministers were not alert to it.'

Arlington had a face like a disgusted frog but wisely held his peace.

'The sooner Danby is back to take the reins again, the better! Where is the man, anyway? Why desert me when I need him most?'

Because you need him most, I thought. *It's his way of reminding you of that.* But I said nothing either.

'You have earned our thanks, Mercurius. A stain on our hospitality can be erased. I want to show my gratitude. Arlington, have we got a bishopric vacant at the moment?'

'Norwich, Your Majesty. But may I point out that Master Mercurius, while admirable in his faith, is not a minister of the Church of England?'

'Stuff and nonsense,' said Charles. 'I'm Supreme Governor of the Church of England. Can't I decide who is a member of the Church and who isn't?'

'It would be … irregular,' Arlington said, but quickly added, 'though no doubt within your powers.'

'Well, I suppose it would only annoy my nephew if I pinch his best clergy,' Charles conceded.

And that is how close I came to being appointed Bishop of Norwich. Of course, being a closet Roman Catholic might have caused me some scruples, and I am fairly certain that my bishop in the Low Countries would have taken the news very badly, but it might have been fun. When I found out where this place Norwich was, I discovered that I would have been the local bishop for the Pastons, which would have given me the opportunity to enjoy the company of Mrs Paston and confuse Mr Paston unutterably with my sermons; but it was not to be, and that is probably for the best.

'Arlington, give Mercurius here some suitable reward. I leave it to you.'

'If I may, Your Majesty,' I said, 'there is one thing I would esteem more than anything else as a reward.'

'Name it,' said Charles.

'I may be thought too tender of heart,' I said, 'but I believed Meg when she said that her brother deceived her. It would be very hard to condemn a young girl when one who should have protected her has used her in this way.'

Charles was chivalrous by nature. He liked pleasing women. 'I understand your feeling, Mercurius, but I cannot interfere in the workings of the courts.'

'Indeed not, Your Majesty. And she will be convicted and sentenced. But Your Majesty can then show her mercy.'

Charles thought this over. 'I'll pardon her on the occasion of my niece's wedding. How's that? Arrange it, Arlington. Just make sure I don't pardon her brother by mistake.'

'There is a great demand for women as wives in our American colonies, Your Majesty,' Arlington reminded him.

'So there is. Well, let's send the murderess there. She'll feel at home among others of her kind. Should we brand her first, or will it make it harder to get someone to take her as a wife?'

'Frankly, Your Majesty, they are so desperate for Englishwomen I do not think it matters one way or the other, but we may as well not take the chance,' answered Arlington.

Dismissed while the King dressed again, Arlington and I walked to his suite.

'Are you looking for a wife?' Arlington asked. 'The King has some unwanted mistresses and would be pleased to equip you with a house and a good living.'

'Thank you,' I replied, 'but I do not think any woman should be compelled to live with me. I am most at home in a library. I am not ready for domesticity.'

Mind you, had I seen some of his discarded mistresses before opening my mouth, I might well have held my tongue.

In the event, when we sailed back to Holland I had a couple of things in my chest that had not come with me. One was a beautiful little Book of Hours from the King's personal library, and the other was a casket containing gold coins. I am not going to say how many there were, but if you know the number of the Beast you would not be far wrong.

I did not tell William of my reward. He was a little put out to discover that we would not be receiving any more secrets from Dawkins. I had feared for that young man, but Pepys was able to shield him from retribution. On the other hand, William was pleased that Van Langenburg had successfully concluded the marriage negotiations. I had expected that he would be disappointed not to receive more cash in the dowry, but he brushed that off.

'I don't want money, Mercurius. I want men. Charles' armies are worth more to me than any amount of money, especially if he is paying them. No, I'll soon have them at my disposal and we'll finally give King Louis a bloody nose. I'd better make the most of it before Uncle James succeeds and tries to undo the whole thing; but he can't undo a marriage.' William clapped me on the shoulder. He probably thought it was manly and playful, but it shook my teeth. 'You've done well, Mercurius. I'm grateful. Bouwman has something for you outside. And now, farewell. Until the next time.'

There won't be a next time, I thought. *I'll enter a monastery if I have to. I've had enough of your "little jobs".*

The "something" was a little brother for Charles' casket. Taken together, I had the equivalent of around nine thousand guilders. [Van der Meer whistled as he wrote this down. He has been treating me with more respect since. I suspect he thinks there may be some left. I'm not going to tell him.]

On arrival at Leiden, I swiftly found a goldsmith who agreed to store my money in his strongroom, less a small amount for immediately necessary expenses, and then presented myself at the University. The Rector greeted me without great enthusiasm until I gave him a letter from the Stadhouder.

'It says here you have done well and have performed the State exemplary service, Mercurius. That will reflect well on the University. Indeed, the Stadhouder says he intends to be present at our next Graduation. It is a signal honour.'

Our university was, at that time, just over a hundred years old, but it liked to ape universities of much longer history. It also had a very strange habit of having rigid declarations or policies with severe punishments attached, which it then tempered by largely disregarding them. For example, we were regularly reminded that full academic dress must be worn to graduations and other university ceremonies, but the fact that they had to keep issuing the reminders shows that it was largely disregarded (except for the law professors, who liked nothing better than parading around like peacocks). I have remarked here that if it had been known that I was a Catholic I would have been discharged, and so I would, but there were lecturers in other faculties who were known to be Catholic and nobody batted an eyelid. And then there was another one, which the Rector was about to raise.

'Mercurius, since you are here, I have something to say to you. You will not find it pleasant, I'm afraid.'

When did I ever where you were concerned?

'You are Master Mercurius. Not Doctor Mercurius. You will know, Mercurius, that we have a firm rule that lecturers in the higher faculties such as theology must have doctorates. Masters may teach in the Artes, of course, but not in the higher faculties.'

The Artes was the faculty of liberal arts or humanities where all our students started. Once they passed there, they could progress to the higher faculties of law, medicine or theology for a higher degree. It was not strictly true that masters could not teach there. They could, but they could not be paid. They could teach "for the sake of experience".

I had been allowed some leeway by the previous Rector because I had studied abroad. I had not told anyone it was in a Catholic seminary, of course, and he did not ask.

'It is high time that you presented and defended a thesis, Mercurius. Get your doctorate, or we will have to move you out of the theology faculty to the Artes.'

God forbid! Some of the theology students were imbeciles, it was true, but I had seen the Artes undergraduates. Some of them could barely fasten their own clothes. I'll swear that if I had taken an ordinary die and wagered that I could throw a seven, some of them would not have taken my bet for fear that I might.

'I can give you two years. Keep me informed on your progress. I have asked Professor Spanheim to find you a suitable supervisor.'

Spanheim was Professor of Theology. He and I did not see eye to eye on a number of matters. He was an arch-conservative and I, as you may have guessed, am not.

I returned to my room feeling utterly dispirited. I had enough money to live on if I resigned, but I liked Leiden. I did not want to leave. But neither did I want to complete a doctorate under Spanheim.

But then I recalled that William had said that if he could do anything for me, I only had to ask; so I wrote reminding him he was "Most Supreme Governor" of the University and asked him how he felt about giving me a doctorate.

As it says in the good book, Matthew, chapter seven, verse seven: "Ask, and it will be given to you."

A NOTE TO THE READER

Dear Reader,

Thank you for reading thus far.

When you write fiction that includes real people, I think you have a responsibility not to blacken their names unduly. A number of historic figures occur in my books, but I hope there is nothing to their detriment. I try to paint a picture consistent with the known history, given a bit of artistic licence.

I thought it might be interesting to quote the main sources I consulted in my research for this book. In alphabetical order of author, they include:

The King's Henchman, by Anthony Adolph

Brief Lives, by John Aubrey

History of His Own Time, by Bishop Gilbert Burnet

The Later Stuarts, by Sir George Clark

Robert Hooke and the Rebuilding of London, by Michael Cooper

William III & Mary II, by Jonathan Keates

The Popish Plot, by John Kenyon

Good, Gratifying and Renowned: A concise history of Leiden University, by Willem Otterspeer

Restoration London, by Liza Picard

The Stuart Princesses, by Alison Plowden

Royal Renegades, by Linda Porter

1666: Plague, War and Hellfire, by Rebecca Rideal

A Plague of Informers, by Rachel Weil

James II, by David Womersley

No doubt there should have been more, but I am a novelist, not an historian.

Mercurius is a reluctant detective, and he is certainly very keen not to involve himself in politics which, he notes, often end with someone dead. While he believes without reservation in life after death, he does not want to be proved right prematurely. Do not be surprised, therefore, if he returns nearer to home for his next case.

I am grateful for the kind and generous reviews of these books, particularly from Dutch people, who have tolerated my inevitable errors, thus proving themselves to be the tolerant and intelligent people Mercurius claims them to be (except his undergraduates, of course).

A brief note on William's title may be in order. William held an office in the Netherlands that I have spelled as Stadhouder. It is often rendered as Stadtholder and sometimes as Stadthouder. In common with many other languages, Dutch harbours some variant spellings in the seventeenth century, but I have used the one I encountered most when researching the first book in this series.

If you have enjoyed this novel I'd be really grateful if you would leave a review on **Amazon** and **Goodreads**. I love to hear from readers, so please keep in touch through **Facebook** or **Twitter**, or leave a message on my **website**.

Dank je wel!

Graham Brack

Sapere Books is an exciting new publisher of brilliant fiction and popular history.

To find out more about our latest releases and our monthly bargain books visit our website:
saperebooks.com